Also by M. J. Fitzgerald

ROPE-DANCER

CONCERTINA

Concertina

M. J. FITZGERALD

Random House New York

Library of Congress Cataloging-in-Publication Data

Fitzgerald, M. J.
Concertina.

I. Title.
PS3556.I834C6   1987   813'.54   86-17846
ISBN 0-394-55801-4

Manufactured in the United States of America
23456789
First Edition

FOR MY MOTHER

CONCERTINA

One late February night, at forty-
one, leaning against the back door of the house that for
the last four years she has shared with her mother who
will die in less than a month, Coriola tilts her head towards
the icy, star-ridden sky, her belly arched like a dome with
a daughter being knit into flesh by her flesh, and her heart
suddenly hammers with recognition of the grain-of-sand
world, hammers with the full strangeness of being creature
and human, beats with awe and fear that on this grain,
smaller than the smallest speck of sand on any seashore,
there could be, there should be, one creature, human,
perched, wandering through years briefer than the blink
of an eyelid, wondering in a time through which the
blink of an eyelid lasts a thousand years. That within the
space of a blink, one creature, human, could, should by
chance change, grow towards this moment, learning to be,
to pass deed and seed, world and word to the puny crea-

ture, human, tossing inside her belly. She tilts her head, and the stars race across the sky, defiant of time, dizzy with eternity, lost in the infinite but for her eyes perceiving their winking, terrible existence; and as suddenly her heart resumes its unobtrusive work, the breathing quietens and like a breath of wind the vision passes, leaving her cold, bereft on the doorstep, wrapping the coat tighter around her frame, turning up the collar, glancing at the mere sky before turning back to the warm kitchen and the familiar chores. Shutting with a rattle of glass the awesome world out, Coriola at forty-one waits for William her lover, the death of her mother, the birth of her daughter; waits for the February to follow until the last, at seventy-five, lying in a hospital bed with her daughter by her side holding a hand made skeletal by the alien life unpicking her flesh.

But at one, sitting up and being fed a paste of solids that maintained her body in life, Coriola threw a mug clear across the room. Her mother, who was washing lettuce at the sink, turned, went and retrieved the yellow beaker and placed it on the tray of the high chair. Seeing that the baby's mouth was finally empty, she stuffed in another mouthful, smiled at it and returned to her task, a silhouette against the light.

The baby hurled the beaker again.

As a child, Coriola was active, perhaps a little hyperactive, although neither particularly intelligent nor sensitive: she simply had to do things, to keep busy. And why not? Her parents were reasonably well off; they could afford, even with the addition of a couple of siblings, the fees for extras such as piano lessons, Brownies, camping. Coriola threw herself into these activities with the same vitality with which as a baby she had hurled objects across space and rolled from one end of the room to the other before she was granted the pleasure of running almost before she could walk and never mind if she fell flat on her face: that grief was short-lived, turned into pleasure by the lifting and being carried in strong arms, sitting astride her father's shoulders surveying the world, and her mother by his side in a heavy big tummy that was a brother who was being made and sometimes kicked to say hello.

"Put your hand here, can you feel?"

"Yes."

"He kicks to say hello; say hello to him."

"Hello," she shouted because he might not hear.

"Don't pick it up, it's dirty."

"Why?"

"Coriola, don't do that."

"Why?"

"We don't like watching you pick your nose."

"Coriola, what are you doing?" Her mother, wheeling the stroller where the one-year-old Stephen sat, turned.

"I'm hot," Coriola at three explained, having pulled her dress over her head, pushing down her pants.

"Coriola, put your clothes back on. You can't wander around the streets with no clothes on."

"Why?"

"Come on, you can take them off as soon as we get home."

"Mummy, look at the faces he's making."
"Don't point your finger like that."
"Why?"
"You can hurt people by doing that."

"You mustn't touch yourself there."
"Why?"
"Do as you're told."
"It feels nice."
"I don't care, you just stop doing it."

"Coriola, don't say that."
"Why? You do."
"Don't do as I do, do as I say."
"Why?"
"Come on, Miss Why, let's get you to school."
"Why?"
"Coriola, will you stop?"
"Why school?"
"Don't you want to write? And read?"
"Yes."
"Well, you go to school to learn to do things."

She learned to skip, swim, dance, ride. It made sense to learn to do things. She learned not to pick her nose, swear, scream, touch herself, have tantrums, hit her brothers, point her finger, take off her clothes in the middle of the street on a hot day but only to strip in the garden to be doused by the sprinkler that went round and round making tiny rainbows against the sun. She learned not to throw beakers across rooms. But whereas the doing of things had a reason—the pleasure of the activity—the not doing was nonsense: why shouldn't she scream, and never mind that she had to put her hands over her ears when her brothers screamed? She wanted to scream sometimes just as much as she wanted to skip or swim. But her vocabulary was limited: all she could say was why, and if the answers did not satisfy her, not profoundly, there was no way she could even say, I am dissatisfied, because she did not know that was what she felt at times. The times were also rainy afternoons when she couldn't go out, though more often there was no apparent reason: the desire to lie on the floor and beat her legs against the ground and yell until she was hoarse and purple in the face would sweep over her, almost irresistible and not often resisted.

At forty she asks herself why she should have wanted to have a tantrum in the first place, what combination of elements and influences had induced such a need to lose control: a mother absorbed by the care of two other children, helpless in the company of a daughter whose behavior was unpredictable, a father remote, stretching an occasional long-fingered hand to ruffle further an unruly mass of hair, hesitating to take and embrace? Had she been jealous of the boys, outward children whose anger always had reasons, in whose noisy games she joined and yet felt separate, amazed by them? Was it the strangeness of it all? She writes the words "dissatisfied," "frustrated," each word conveying something, neither saying everything, not even when "unhappy" is added and the three words act in counterpoint; it is as if the words merely push against a mass, shifting but not altering, and the mass itself remains unknowable: why is she unhappy, frustrated, dissatisfied?

And Coriola at forty, not yet pregnant, not even knowing she wants a child, compelled perhaps only by the emptiness of the mild November afternoon to remember and record, remembers holding her father's hand, the light playing with her mother's features, Peter's kite tugging in the first swoop towards the blue air, Stephen and her giggling, Peter climbing into her bed early in the morning, soft warm limbs so tiny and his hands pulling her hair. She remembers watching rain slide down the windowpane and her stillness in a house that was too quiet: had she been alone? She had been, perhaps for a fraction of a second, perhaps for hours, totally absorbed in the game of rain and can hear, in the memory she strains back to that time, nothing. Or is it a dream? It has the quality of silence that dreams have. She remembers walking down the street pulling at the bushes that protected the houses, humming; chanting as she played hopscotch with the irregular slabs of stone on the pavement; throwing a ball against the wall, pirouetting before catching it. Were those moments of happiness? Coriola asks, sitting at the kitchen table. And even as she writes, she wonders at the labels she is slapping onto experiences that elude definition. She glances at the plane tree that darkens the room while grey deepens into black, and when she hears her mother moving, switching on the light, walking to the bedrooms to turn down the beds, drawing the curtains in the sitting room, coughing, a harsh rasp against the back of the throat, she puts away the notebook to prepare their evening meal.

2
___

Coriola at six asked, knowing that
the answers were there, she simply did not know them:
by asking she would receive. At school she liked to play
with numbers and learned that two and two make four,
that if she added four ten times, she got to forty, and if
she took two away, it was thirty-eight, that strange hybrid
number that seemed hardly even, containing as it did
simply two nineteens, like the twenty-six composed of
two thirteens, or the thirty-four that opened merely to the
seventeen. The symmetry of adding even number to even
number satisfied her, but the three, the five, the seven
she found disturbing, the one left over made her uneasy,
she liked only their regular return to the familiar evens,
ten, twelve, fourteen, and frequently skipped the uneven
nine, fifteen, twenty-one, the inevitable encounter with
numbers that complicated the addition, played havoc with
the orderliness of the multiplication, defeated any

neat conclusion to the division. Only when she discovered the descending scale in the addition of nines, from eighteen to eighty-one, and a new, visual symmetry in the mirrorlike quality of the two numbers did she learn to love the nine. She hated fractions; she liked whole, round numbers: it felt like a violence to her to have half a two, one of five, as if something essential were being taken away. She fought and refused to submit to the fragmenting of numbers and became a poor student of math after the age of ten.

She learned to read and write, though it took her some years to come to terms with the accumulation of fragments that made up letters and words: was it not absurd that words turned to worlds, that an arbitrary letter should be repeated at random, wander and wonder to form an equally imprecise word, a seed that had no fullness, needing always another word to change it, never complete, unlike numbers that stood, even the three, precise and definite, with no hesitation and no ambiguity?

But as the precision of numbers dissolved in points and commas, words began to merge into sentences and paragraphs that led her gently by the hand through descriptions and stories, and she forgot the incongruities of noun and verb and began to play with words—she bears the bears; he left the lift and turned left; it is right to write with the right hand; the word is flat, and the world is fat; the bored hole bored Jack—laughing secretly at the game, becoming by the age of twelve a voracious reader and a writer of rhymes, reaching to the tantalizing similarity hidden in words, incapable of resisting the possibility that each word was analogue, that to sow was in some profound way also to sew, that to see was to saw.

At thirteen Coriola walked down the street, a big, rather overdeveloped child, and smiled at everyone, looking them straight in the eye.

"Coriola, don't smile at that man."

"Why?"

"He'll think you're flirting."

"What's flirting?"

"To smile and look men straight in the eye."

"But . . ."

"You'll understand soon enough. For now, just don't do it."

"But I want to smile at everyone. And no one looks at anyone, they always slide their eyes away. I don't like it."

"People misunderstand, Coriola."

"What do they misunderstand? I don't understand."

And she didn't. Why should anyone misunderstand a smile? How could a smile . . . A smile is miles and miles. A vial of smiles, a vile smile. Can there be a vile smile? She looked up the word, saw grin, leer, and was bewildered. It was as if, she confided to her diary when puberty hit and she was reeling from the effects, as if, as if . . . Oh, the despair of discovering nothing is as it seems.

Coriola changed: she practiced looking at men, at people, sideways without smiling, afraid that her features would be misinterpreted, that she would be smirking or leering, that she couldn't grin. She practiced looking over their shoulders at their right ear, but without turning her head to follow the look.

"Coriola, look at people you are being introduced to."

"But . . ."

"And smile, can't you? You look as if you've got a squint."

She was to hate ears for the rest of her life, until at seventy-five, on the day she was taken to hospital, an orderly carried her, light as a feather, in his arms to the bed. He was a boy, as all men were to her by then, and by the time they reached the bed on the sixth floor she would have liked to touch the delicate skin of his ear and feel the pliable cartilage. She thought how absurd it was to be enchanted by an ear and lay exhausted, knowing herself a mass of bones in a carrier of skin, as he drew up the light blanket over her knees. She smiled straight into his eyes, her last friend who would come and occasionally sit by her in the white afternoons of her dying. Even after the short forays into movement were denied and the bed became her home, it helped her to look at the ears of those who came in hurried or lingering visits to the other white beds. She noted the varied structure of this most superfluous part of the body, mused through the lassitude at the persistence of discovery, the pleasure she could still feel, and took out the notebook to record the rewards and absurdities of dying.

But at fifteen bewilderment stunted her growth, pressed down on her, made her square and tubby when most genes in her chemical makeup dictated that she should grow to at least five foot nine.

"Coriola, what is the matter with you?"

"Nothing."

"You've hardly said a word in the last week. Where's my wonderful chatterbox, eh?"

"Leave me alone."

"You're eating too much, not taking enough exercise, always on your bed reading. What's the matter with you?"

"I want to give up the dance class, I'm too fat."

"I don't want to do the piano anymore, it's boring."

"I hate riding, I hate it."

In fact, she had a painful, terrible crush on the riding instructress. In the ordinary way, Coriola would have gone up to her and said, "I want to give you a kiss." It was, after all, exactly what she wanted to do. She wanted to touch her hair, which was brilliantly fair and not a bird's nest like her own. She wanted, she needed to go up to her and say, "I love you." Next time she returned with the most advanced students, bright-eyed from galloping in the hills, Coriola would take the rein, give her an arm to help her get off the lithe back, and say, "I love you." It was very simple, really. There was no complication in Coriola's emotion beyond the complexity of the emotion itself. Not yet, at least, though notice how instead of saying to her mother, "I love her and I want to kiss her," she said she hated riding, she hated it. Why did she choose—did she choose?—not to tell her mother what her feelings for the riding instructress were? Why not tell everyone? What was the mechanism that drove her to secrecy, she who by nature had no secrets in her? Did her mother say or do something that marked the child?

Of course, a parent's mere existence marks a child,

every word spoken in a bewildering world affects it, who is forced to alter its nature without understanding, Coriola writes at forty, glancing at her mother asleep across the room from the desk, in the armchair lit by the standard lamp. At seventy-five, Coriola smiled. Look at the number of times the mother had said "Don't do that" to Coriola. What could Coriola do? She wanted to throw the beaker across the room, but when after the third throw the mother's voice changed from the most exquisite sound—for Coriola: anyone who overheard it might have criticized it for its flatness and lack of texture—to a high-pitched, impatient "Don't do that, Coriola," what could Coriola do? She could not, yet, go and pick up the beaker and enjoy alone the movement of throwing, the subsequent noise of plastic on linoleum, the pleasant way it bounced and rolled. She was dependent on her mother, who did not always see the game, who got tired of the game before Coriola, whose mind was on the latest quarrel with her husband and the lovemaking to come—should she wear the silk underwear he gave her for Christmas or not wear anything at all?—whose body was weary from the constant demands of another existence totally dependent on her own, so weary she was not sure she wanted to make love at all—but she had been brought up with the theory that men have to have it and believed that the quarrels had arisen because of her unresponsiveness; in fact it had nothing to do with her and everything to do with a power play that was taking place in the office, about which he was unable to speak. She knew she was the one who must make the effort: she didn't, consciously, resent this, and instead thought she resented the dependence of Coriola on her; Coriola who would sit there with a mouth full of food for minutes at a time, without swallowing, throwing the beaker across the room. It was enough to drive a saint to fury, and she was no saint. She didn't choose to have this child as she would choose to have her siblings. The conception happened because she was twenty-three and he was twenty-five, and girls meet boys, and she liked to feel his arms around her, and he, guiltily, to finger farther and farther inside her, and once they got that far they couldn't back out, and anyway that is what happens all the time, everyone gets married, unless they are really ugly or "odd," like the physics and history teachers at the boarding school she went to until she was eighteen, whose main shared characteristic was vast flat posteriors, and who had shared a flat since the world had begun.

She did enjoy it, the deflowering and so on, until she got too big for comfort and then when the baby arrived she really went off it. And now they were constantly quarreling. But tonight would change everything—she just hoped they wouldn't wake the baby with all the carry-on, she was quite noisy when they'd been at it for a while, she was going to have to quiet herself, and that alone was an almost insurmountable problem. So she shook the lettuce more violently than she needed to and turned an impatient face, a high-pitched voice on her daughter.

"Stop it," she screamed, and the words, spoken from the necessity of the mother's nature, though not necessarily from the sequence of reasons Coriola invents for her at forty, in the silence broken by her mother's open-mouthed breathing in sleep, the words, Coriola writes, altered the child. And each time the one clashed with the other, Coriola changed: she changed as imperceptibly as the death of trees or the alterations in a landscape buffeted by winds and rain, heat and cold. Yet what can a mother do if a child will go on sucking its thumb, putting its fingers inside its panties, pointing at strangers, approaching a man, a woman and saying, "I want to kiss you," throwing beakers? She cannot very well let it behave in such an antisocial way, can she? It is merely the socialization of a wild creature, is it not? It's all part of growing up, of life, natures must be changed to fit in with the natures of others. Isn't it, isn't it? What do "must," "should," "ought" do here? We try forever to construct a different world, and those words are the brick and mortar, Coriola writes, proud of the phrase. At forty-one she knows that the mother, too, changed, that the alterations were mutual, that there cannot be encounter without clash, that clash is a word, a harsh, unforgiving word for the shifts between two placed in each other's orbit. At forty, before her mother falls ill and the pattern of their relationship alters beyond recognition, Coriola cannot yet conceive of that compli-cation, believing still, though not acknowledging the be-lief, in the childish myth of unalterable parenthood: the mother, struggle as she may, cannot remember her child-hood except as endless summer, gold and green. Coriola at forty-one knows Coriola at forty did not allow her mother to remember any day before her birth, because she would have had to forgive if she had known the mother suffered childhood as she herself did, although in a different con-text—with a mother who was constantly ill, two brothers and a severe father who, when the mother died, sent her to live with a young red-haired aunt, with whom she stayed for a number of years before going to boarding school when the aunt married and left the country. Coriola at seventy-five, knowing much more, tosses suddenly in bed one night, unable to wipe from her mind the figure and the luminous brown eyes of a young man, standing next to a tall dark-haired girl with troubled, frowning features.

3
___

The accumulation of don't, mustn't, shouldn't was in any case merely the origin of Coriola's first secrecy at fifteen. The determinants were other: had there not been two events in her short life, she might not have thought that the crush on the riding instructress was among the things that should not happen and the fact that it had was no excuse. And even so, her realization was nebulous, less knowledge than instinct, an inarticulate shrinking from the possible consequences of revelation, of going up plainly to her mother and saying, "I love her, Mummy; help me, her hair is so blond, and it shines like the sun, and her smile is warm, and I want to be with her always."

Because once she had. She had gone to her mother once, aged ten, with a poem, a poem to a child in her class, a small dainty creature of red curls and dimples with whom she had made friends: they laughed rapturously at everything, retreated to Coriola's room or Melissa's and lay on the floor among the books, *Heidi*, *Little Women*, *The Call of the Wild*, *Kim*, *Alice*; the comics, *Superman*, *Mickey Mouse*, in inexplicable paroxysms of joy. They walked everywhere hand in hand, their arms around each other, giggling tee-hee-hee, talking, talking, revealing themselves to each other as completely as Coriola would ever reveal herself—she's horrible, he's great, I love her, I'm crazy about him, I'm going to be famous, I'm going to be an actress, I'll have lots of children. You can marry Stephen, and I'll marry Mike, and we'll get married on the same day, we'll have a double wedding, and then we can both have twins. I'm going to run away tonight from that horrible cow, do you want to come? I wish I had your hair, shall I brush it for you? They nuzzled each other's bodies as puppies are wont to do. They nuzzled each other's hearts as humans are wont to do. It was Coriola's most joyous interlude in a life that at forty appears to stretch forever, tauter and thinner like an elastic band that refuses to snap and be broken.

"Don't say things like that," the mother snapped when she read the poem.

"Like what?"

"Your mustn't say I love to touch you."

"Why? She has soft cheeks and soft hair, and I do."

"Yes, but you mustn't say it."

"Why?"

"Then you must say I love to touch your hair."

"Why?"

"It sounds better."

"Really?"

"Do you have to write a poem to her?"

"She's my best friend."

"Yes, well."

"Shall I write a poem to you?"

"Yes, why don't you do that."

"And to Daddy?"

"That would be lovely, I'm sure he'd like that."

"Can I say I love to touch you?"

And the mother got up abruptly, not knowing what to say. The child seemed to have no instinct for what was right and what was wrong, she was sure she had never been like that, couldn't she sense it was not right to say such a thing?

All Coriola sensed was her mother's disapproval. All she did was not show her mother the next poem she wrote in which she felt the need to say I love to touch you: the poem was to a boy for whom she undressed in the greenhouse, and who undressed for her, at around the same time, perhaps the spring after, as she walked down the street smiling and looking people straight in the eye. The boy was a couple of years younger, and she undressed because she wanted to see him undressed. Being ignorant and incapable of sex, they never had sex. But they did a lot of touching, and Coriola, as was her way, wrote a poem about it. And although the sentence "I love to touch you," written for her curly-headed friend Melissa, who had moved from the district and become a stranger, was completely different from the "I love to touch you" written for Desmond, whose teeth stuck out, whose nose was invaded by ridiculous freckles that played right into the hands of the mischief in the eyes, Coriola only had those words. Years later she was to return to those two poems, one tucked into the back of *The Wind in the Willows* which she had outgrown soon after and forgotten at the far end of the long bookshelf until she came to pack her belongings for storage when she finally left home at twenty-five; the other glued like a frontispiece into her first diary. At thirty-seven, returning home, though the house was the small one her mother had moved to after the death of her husband, Coriola took the objects of her childhood out of storage and filled the narrow room. She found the two poems and wondered that the expression of two fundamentally different emotions and physical experiences should have been identical. At forty they determine her into a search for what will explain the nature of each emotion, the difference between them, the need to say and the necessity therefore to have, create, invent the right words and not perpetrate the confusion of identical verb, to touch, for the laying of skin against skin that expresses as many different emotions as—as there are greens in the world, she thinks, pausing one spring morning in the common on the way to the hospice where her mother is, dying. She looks at the trees, the shrubs, the grass, and thinks perhaps, like the color, touch should be prefixed: a spring touch, a weeping-willow touch, a beech touch. Coriola at seventy-five laughed in her sleep, knowing one word was, after all, enough, and that the search through subtlety was doomed to failure. But nonetheless necessary.

She was discovered by her father, standing without any clothes on in front of the tall rubber plant. Desmond was still clothed, and his hands were cupping her breasts, already heavy, good for suckling, a mother's breasts rather than the upturned breasts of a virgin. There was no sexual excitement, though a good deal of pleasure. Desmond was curious, and his curiosity renewed itself frequently. He felt after a while that though he had touched and held and stroked and even nibbled at the breasts, he still did not know them and needed to explore them again, rather as he had handled and chewed on bright colored objects not so long before. And he liked to see the new hairs that hid the mound curl around his finger. Coriola was fascinated by the reaction of the prepubertal cock, which would straighten at odd moments, unprompted.

The father was furious and was never to realize the fury that made him take a swipe at Desmond, which landed the child on the cement floor and cracked his skull so that he was unconscious for twenty-four hours, though fully recovered within a month, contained a wealth of contradictory elements of which anger against Desmond was perhaps the least important, and the most important, because the most frightening and therefore the one most likely to be suppressed, was his own very definite sexual arousal.

"What the hell . . . ?"

Coriola could only look at Desmond's pale face on the pale cement floor.

"You hurt him."

"Put your clothes back on, you little slut."

It was not the moment to ask, as she usually did, "What does it mean?" She looked it up later in the dictionary, when she had been locked in her room and her father downstairs in the sitting room, was swallowing his third whisky, trembling, from anger still but even more from fear that he had killed the child.

"Slovenly woman" the dictionary said. And slovenly meant a person of careless, untidy habits. Did untidiness warrant such a pale face on such a hard floor, and being locked in her room? In what way had she been careless? She thought of the words, and they didn't make sense. Untidiness up to that moment had been the havoc she seemed incapable of not creating in her room and was connected with her mother's invariable rebuke, "You live in a pigsty," impatiently picking up socks, blouses, skirts, books. The words echoed with her mother's tone. At school, on the other hand, she was always praised for the tidiness of her presentation: her large regular script was a pleasure to read, her teachers agreed in chorus. She was never, unlike Desmond and Melissa, careless or untidy in her work. A good solid student without a spark of originality but with all the qualities that please instructors because they do not draw attention to the pupil. The teachers could dismiss her from their minds after the praise and turn to Desmond, who was bright but never did anything unless blackmailed or threatened, or Melissa, who, at a different school, was growing too pretty to bother with studying: it was much more pleasant to pretend not to be waiting for the boys to go past her, dazzled by her dainty ways, or to enjoy the next anonymous message passed to her along the whole length of the classroom among murmured giggles. "I love you," it said, and Melissa would blush and look around to discover who had sent it. Sometimes teachers would confiscate the piece of paper folded into a little square, but it was obvious by the way they turned away that they understood the inevitability of it and were indulgent. In the staff room the chat among the men alighted on her—"Give her a few years . . ." —and took off again, apprehensive of the attraction she exerted with no deliberation. The men imagined her learning, half wished they could teach her, and one, Fanian, could not go near her for the thrust of his craving for her and his image of her against a wall, coltish legs apart, arms in an arc above her head, wrists tied, eyes shut and red hair in disarray, wearing a vest and white cotton pants with blue mice scuttling across: he had seen them as she did a handstand in the playground almost a year before, and buried his desire in the body of the slim plain woman he was going to marry at the end of the summer term, before he moved to a new job as head of English in a large boys' school.

Coriola at thirteen looked out of the window in her room at the first large drops making perfect circles on the fishpond her father had just finished building, and puzzled over the word slut. She liked it, it sounded definite, decisive, tidy. Nicer than slovenly, which was certainly an untidy word, sliding in and out of the mouth and getting blurred. Yet she was no nearer understanding what it meant and why, therefore, she was locked in her room and Desmond was lying in the hospital while both fathers sat downstairs drinking and the mothers, stunned, sat by the child's bed willing him out of unconsciousness.

Desmond's father was to be rather proud of his son's early experimentation: that he himself should have been so lucky, put away as he had been in a boarding school when he was nine, his mother pale and tight-lipped in her silks, and he completely bereft in the tepid dormitory, but without crying, manly, imagining himself with his father's mustache, walking erect through a life at his beck and call. He had seen many boys' organs, at rest in showers, at play with others, but had never felt any great keenness to be touched. Secretly he now regretted that he hadn't, after many years of discreet philandering through a life his father would have called disappointing had he not died years before. He wondered whether the sensation might not be at least a little different. He even occasionally imagined being unzipped by a faceless man with strong young hands. It helped him to make love to his wife, whose freckles, red hair and mischievous mien Desmond had inherited, if she turned to him after he had been indulging with some girl or other during the lunch hour and felt guilty enough not to be able to reject her advances.

Desmond himself remembered his stay in the hospital with great satisfaction and entertained friends regularly throughout his life by the retelling of the event, which gradually accumulated detail and information that, though not accurate, were precisely remembered. His liking for big breasts became his main source of sexual excitement and led him, before he chose a career, to explore the underworld of pornography. He specialized in the photography of large-breasted women, all of whom he tried to seduce until one, bold as brass, seduced him, and he discovered the pleasure of knowing who could make him laugh in and out of bed and who, if she was jealous of the others he was handling with the camera, never showed it. By the time Coriola left home at twenty-five, he had embarked on work as a private detective, had married and walked the streets by his wife's side, wheeling the first pram, proud of the sideways looks of men on her, who, perched on stiletto heels, was incapable of taking a full stride: his pleasure in her walk, her ass, her tits was constant, and he would remain semierect sometimes all afternoon in anticipation of seeing her in the evening.

If only Melissa had remained in the district, to explain to Coriola the necessity of it, of meeting in greenhouses and toilets, undressing in front of boys and risking the wrath of parents who no longer wished to remember: Coriola's father had stood outside doors and looked through keyholes at his mother, his aunts, the frequent women visitors. He had climbed on their laps to feel their breasts against his back, his arms, his cheek, pressing his face to hear the heartbeat, with two fingers in his mouth. By the time he was Coriola's age he had touched a woman he did not know was young, she seemed so old to his twelve years, who had taken his hand and placed it between her closed legs and surprised him by the warmth and texture of skin, so like the skin of the childish cock he had always fondled. He was shocked by the feel of hair, it set his heart racing: he pulled back his hand and immediately regretted it. But he had chosen to forget and was to bury the latest episode so deeply he retained only the vaguest memory of it within a few years of their move to another part of town, to an almost identical house. As he never remembered his dreams, he had no idea of the number of times he had a nighttime ejaculation from a dream in which his child's naked body, topped by an indistinct face framed in a beehive of coarse black hair with red ribbons trailing, stood exposed to his gaze. He was never close to Coriola.

Although that was perhaps her fault, Coriola thinks at forty, cleansing her skin, preparing to go out and meet William, who will try to kiss her. She would like to cancel the thought she has written only a few weeks before, that her father, even in his dreams, may have desired her. It is an invention. It is the futile search for reasons, to explain what perhaps had no explanation. There was no reason, she thinks. She and her father were never close, the fact was as arbitrary as the conjunction of seed and seed that led to her birth rather than the birth of another. She would like to wipe the thought, draw a line through the words, substitute another set of words that would bring her father close to her, but she knows, as she applies mascara, that the words have to remain, that the explanation also will remain, because it is, however arbitrary, the explanation she has been compelled to create. She refuses to ask herself why she should have been so compelled, or why the fact that she was should be any justification for it.

She wipes off a smudge, pulls on the sheer tights, turns in front of the mirror, cheating herself into the belief that it is to make the dress fall properly over the hips, but knowing, as she adjusts a pleat and wonders whether the earrings she has planned to wear are the best ones, that the mirror is the instrument of contradictory reassurances, without which she would be incapable of leaving her narrow room to meet the stranger who entered her life on the February day she accompanied her mother to the hospice. Eventually she is ready to switch off the light and enter the cold night: the glare from the full moon fades the distant stars and lights the earth, and William waits.

4

_A_ teenager's secrets are quite transparent, when the secret is kept not out of necessity for privacy but from bewilderment, Coriola writes: even her mother noticed Coriola's crush on the riding instructress and laughed, not really understanding, misreading. She called it a pash after her own experience at boarding school, where it happened all the time and was harmless, absolutely harmless: if she was honest, what else had she felt for her young aunt after she had been sent to boarding school? And for those girls whose smile could lift the day into the air she walked on, whose indifference crushed her with terrifying misery, as if the full emptiness of life were reflected in the empty eyes turned to her, not acknowledging her. How very silly it all was, she thought, picking up her daughter from her riding lesson.

"You have got a pash on her, haven't you?" liking her suddenly much more, the resentment fading or being buried still more deeply, down, down, below sympathy, interest, curiosity. She remembered Harriet, Denise . . . she remembered Marian, and she thought, at least she won't humiliate herself, get involved with boys, pursue them. Yes, it is better, a harmless crush, she thought, parking the car, following her awkward daughter into the house.

Pash did not seem the right word to Coriola. What she felt sliding untidily between pleasure and anguish needed a soft, long, blurred word like slovenly: love. But she could not say that to her mother, so she simply said that there would be no need for her mother to come and pick her up if she were to get a bicycle; she begged to have the one that was being sold by one of the boys at the stable who had saved enough to buy a motorcycle with a roaring engine to desecrate the silence.

The riding instructress, a pleasant woman whose long-standing relationship with a local civil servant had come to an end quite abruptly when her lover was transferred and then announced she was marrying the head of the department in her new office, had strong sexual urges that riding did not satisfy. She looked at the square teenager whose legs were already almost as long as her own, whose grey eyes were set so wide apart they gave her a per-manently perplexed expression, whose rare smile was lovely; she was a good horsewoman, the riding instruc-tress thought. And she thought, why not, when she saw the look Coriola was trying not to put into words. She took her to her bed, undressed her and touched her and said to her, "I love you." But she did not mean the same by the words as Coriola meant when she said it back, "Oh I love you, I love you."

The riding instructress meant, you are young, your body is not beautiful perhaps, but the skin is soft, the mound tender and the juices fresh and unsullied. You satisfy me. But all that would have taken too long to say, and in fifteen minutes she had to give a lesson to a peaky boy who was as terrified of sitting astride a horse as she might be hanging from a branch over a ravine. She preferred to teach Coriola how to touch: she knew by now, having taken to bed other teenagers, the right combination of gentleness and ruthlessness. It was like training a horse, to get it to do what you want, you pull hard on the reins but also stroke its neck. The words were merely a calculated stroke. How could Coriola know that the words spoken, which were identical to her own, meant something completely different? To her, as is the way with teenagers, the words meant that the sun shines through you, that beauty has no better incarnation than your eyes, your hair, your walk, your being; that if I don't say it again and again to myself and to you, I shall burst; that my heart is in my mouth, my heart is in your hand; that love, that you, have become god. Someone should have told Coriola, lying on the single mattress in the hut near the stables after the instructress had buckled her belt, pulled on her boots and gone, and the little room darkened, someone should have told her, Coriola writes at forty as the wind whips the house and the new year weeps its way into time, that love is not anything but word.

Still, it was spoken, and Coriola grew and slimmed down. For a while she was under the illusion that love restores simplicity, that everything, encompassed by that word, is indeed as it seems. She had no need to hurl beakers across rooms: she had all the words, all the words in all the languages, and everyone understood, or would have understood if she had not felt a necessary privacy that was not shame. Words poured out of her, each word a number, an exact expression of what she meant. The earth stood firm beneath her feet. She looked up words in dictionaries to find definitions and wrote long poems to her beloved. She riffled through anthologies for words, verses, sentences that would express it and was surprised to find so many had written her words already, though she will not be later, at forty, before the late winter days when her life begins, miraculously, to be refashioned.

She thinks that it is the communal burden, the absurd search for someone to love, the absurd emotion that is the cause of all events, its presence perennial spring, its absence permanent winter. Love makes the world go around. The cliché repeats itself in her head: she has a picture of it, not unlike the mechanism of interlocking wheels in a watch, the phrase going around, yes, but in the opposite direction from love itself, as if the repeated phrase is a series of obstacles that love has to surmount before it can make the world go around. As if she cannot accept the simplicity, yield to its demands and follow in the wake of a world that goes around by love, be part of it, and she is using the very phrase to erect a barrier between the world, moved by love, and herself, at a standstill from lack of it. Her mother is downstairs, fussing about the house, restless with the beginnings of the illness. Next week is the appointment with the doctor, postponed again and again.

She wonders, knowing from the degree of noise that her mother wants company: for the last four years there has been a special cough, a particular sound in her movements that has indicated her mother has finished with solitude for the day, and Coriola has joined her, to share her own solitude; she wonders tonight why it is that their companionship is not enough for either of them, giving their life together an edge of bickering, a tight-lipped meanness, a silence that weighs on them and from which neither can escape.

At sixteen she wrote out verses in her large clear script and left them in the hut with a flower, a stalk, a stone, for the riding instructress to find, before cycling home through seasons heavy with the scents of summer and the fresh pipings of spring. She did not know that the riding instructress frequently did not bother to read the words but shredded them quickly so there would be no evidence of what was going on.

"We'll have to stop your lessons."

"Why?"

"People talk."

"What?"

"People. They talk."

"Who? So?"

"Don't look at me like that. People will notice."

"Don't speak to me like that. People."

"You must not go on coming here. People talk. You are under age. I've seduced you."

"What?"

"I'm a pervert, a deviant. Bent."

"What does it mean?"

"I've seduced you Coriola. Don't you understand?"

"What does it mean?"

"You're as thick as two planks."

"But I love you."

The riding instructress had met a woman with a girl-child and was, she told herself and the woman, very much in love; she meant that here was the prospect of a domestic setup for which she had looked for some years. The woman was not too demanding, reasonably solvent and comfortable to be with, the child gave her the illusion of a motherhood she was in fact incapable of exercising. And Coriola talked so much, for goodness sake, with such intensity, always wanting to be honest, to speak the truth. What is truth, the riding instructress asked herself, getting up impatiently from the chair in the hut where Coriola sat. Coriola sat because the earth trembled beneath her feet. She had, until the exchange, been standing behind her lover, enchanted by the highlights in her hair that she did not know were man-made.

The complications are infinite: even the movement, the rising impatiently, the words she spoke in her head, what is truth, were they not to hide the guilt? After all, she had seduced the child, hadn't she, hadn't she?

Well, she had, according to her lights and to her upbringing, a strict one in a family full of men, Coriola writes, struggling to understand, struggling through the whisper of pen on paper, against the sudden silence of the house her mother has left, locking the door to her room, taking the key with her. There had been a pale mother and her mother's much younger sister, the only person who laughed and giggled with her; the person through whom she had either learned of, or simply learned her sexual, her emotional inclinations, even though they had never so much as laid a finger on each other except for the acceptable hugs and kisses of affectionate sisters—only the child knew unassuaged cravings from these hugs. It was only in retrospect, years later, well after she had added Rita to her string of seductions and the relationship with Rita's mother had disintegrated, that the riding instructress recognized that the central component of sexual excitement was the guilt induced as much by a repeated fantasy of female incest as by the breaking of rules; and it is only Coriola at forty, not yet secure in love, who wonders whether the components were inherent or had been chiseled by the effect on the riding instructress of one personality, her father's? Her mother's? some strange man who had exposed himself to her when she was too young to understand her own fear? her brother? Or had it been the witnessing of a constant and sly cruelty in her father towards her mother, defenseless and ill? Was she, by loving women, trying to redeem her father from his arbitrary dislike of her mother, or trying to protect women from the possibility of a parallel cruelty in a relationship with a man? Or trying to protect herself from it? Or was it, more simply, the constant search, in the desirability of another woman's body, for confirmation of her own desirability, the proof that if she could feel like touching another so like her, the other must feel like touching her?

And what Coriola said, that she had no idea what seduced meant, was it truth? Why had she been so careful to arrange independence by begging her mother for a bicycle just a few weeks before the seduction in the hut? Surely at sixteen she knew what seduced meant? She had come across the word, but what she experienced, Coriola finds herself explaining to William, pacing the room as spring rain washes the house, what she experienced did not correspond to the meaning of the word as she had learned it, and like a poor mathematician, she could not adapt theorems to a number of problems, the same word to a variety of experience. She had been learning fast and had been quite adept at applying terms from one book to another. But what book might a seventeen-year-old read that described the seduction of a girl by a woman? And is not the leap from read experience to life experience as difficult as that from understanding of speech by a child to the child taking to itself the word to articulate its own perceptions?

Even so, does the fact that Coriola at sixteen had no idea of the permutations of seduction actually preclude the possibility that it had been Coriola, young and fresh-bodied, who had seduced the riding instructress? Is there anything more seductive than youth, adoring?

In the end, of course, yes. Many things. Most important is domestic contentment. At least, it was for the riding instructress, who knew in her heart of hearts that young bodies can always be replaced by other young bodies, especially in her kind of job. But if she let this chance slip, there might only be a diminishing succession of young bodies on a single bed in a dark hut near the stables. She wasn't, as men and women have said before and will say again in endless chorus, she wasn't getting any younger.

Is it not simplification to point to anything and say, ah, that is why she is as she is? There are other elements, further complications, a series of causes and effects that recede into a horizon of mystery the more clearly the gaze is trained on a life. Like Coriola, like everyone, what the riding instructress knew often contradicted what she was, and in any case she was not any one thing, but a mass being acted upon by what she could never understand, by what could not be understood. Had she not seduced Coriola only because Coriola did not in fact respond enough to the inclinations, emotions and contradictions that are abbreviated and simplified under the term lesbian? If Coriola had, and if the riding instructress had actually found in her a permanent companion, would the fact that Coriola had been only fifteen when they became lovers have mattered? Coriola loved the instructress with a love that was to have no parallels in intensity and depth, yet, throughout the eighteen months they lay and touched each other, never did her own pleasure go beyond the pleasure of giving pleasure. Her body, opened and sprawled on the cot in the hut, remained locked and secret. That it should have been so, is that not as mysterious as the drive by a woman to seek another woman? Coriola at seventy-five wondered whether it had been the aberration that beauty always induces, misconstrued for homosexuality where labels are used to fix something that keeps shifting premises and perspective and words. She waited with trembling hands and beating heart for a young girl who came to clean her windows every month, who looked down on her with unconscious condescension and smiled at the old dear who was stunned anew by the structure of her face and the shape of her hands. She was the daughter of the son of pretty Melissa, from whom perhaps she had inherited the traits that set Coriola's heart beating, though Coriola did not know and never would know this particular coincidence. But she offered her cups of tea and specially bought cakes so that she might be with her a little longer and savor the way her wrist widened into her forearm and her eyebrows thickened.

Beauty is the downfall of both ages, and youth adds itself to make the downfall more humiliating for the old. And in between youth and old age the power of it is kept at bay at times. At times it cannot be avoided, the staring at beauty in the shape of man or woman . . . and no, it is not the same, beauty, as physical perfection: the riding instructress was not beautiful, no advertising agency or school of modeling or even pornographic magazine would have looked at her twice, though they would employ Coriola later, after the age of twenty-five, Coriola thought: she wanted to touch the window-cleaning girl's face and feel the cheekbones under the pure skin. But she was seventy-five and already the cancer was making her hands shake. And a few months later she would be carried to her bed by Desmond, whose ears she longed to touch as much as she had longed to touch the girl's skin, whose name she would be pleased to know, remembering the red-haired boy whose ears stuck out, who she did not know had died slowly and painfully in a nearby bed not long before she made of the hospital her last home; Desmond, the orderly who became within thirty years potbellied, bad-tempered, incapable of keeping his eyes and then his hands away from the fresh skin of his wife's much younger sister and was a tyrant to his daughter, whose only comfort was the pretty red-haired aunt.

What other point could there have been for the riding instructress in the seduction of Coriola but the worship of beauty? Sex? Of course. Just sex? Coriola at forty ponders the question during William's unsatisfactory first night with her, and when he's left, writes it down thus: Who's fooling whom? Which comes first, sex or beauty? Can there be one without the other? The riding instructress had sex with the mother of the girl-child for the rest of her life; but when the child was fifteen, she worshipped at the altar of youth and beauty and added another to her string of seductions.

But what can explain the ambiguity that was the central component of the riding instructress's emotional makeup? When her young aunt had eventually married and stopped the unconscious flirting with her large niece, the riding instructress, alone with her pale mother, as old as Coriola was when she lay in the hut and the earth trembled, had her first affair with a married teacher whose son had introduced her to riding, had deflowered her among the wood shavings in his father's carpentry shop, and for whom she felt an irritation when his lips sought her body and he thrust himself into her, but only after she had been kissed by his mother. The excitement of that first kiss renewed itself, was surpassed in subsequent encounters, in the lessons of touch she had received and taught, almost invariably with women who, unlike her, could and did find their greater satisfaction with men: was it then their greater fault, who sought her, who yielded to her?

As for Coriola's bid for independence through a bicycle, it was the term that she had a pash that was the final straw in the accumulation of clashes between her and her mother, who was undergoing an intense involvement with the head of English at her son's school. It isn't until months after her mother dies in the spring of Coriola's forty-first year, Coriola inserts the last time she writes, after feeding her daughter whose head lies heavy in the crook of her left arm, that she can fit that particular piece in the puzzle of her mother's life, that she can fit so many pieces, that she must remove and change some of the pieces in her life which she has forced into a place where they did not fit, knowing now the pattern of her mother's life, how it began long before her own birth, in her mother's teens, in a child's room; how it was halted by marriage, resumed and how it finally ended as Coriola at seventeen was being sick on the side of the road. She knows the letters, she has seen and committed to fire the hidden cache of photographs, brother and sister standing in front of their parents, staring into the camera, the brother posing for the lens in a portrait that showed clearly the impenetrable innocence of his large luminous eyes. She knows the letters, the elegant script of the schoolboy that betrayed no trace of a personality, the letters measured, upright, the *i*'s dotted, the *t*'s crossed, capitals exactly half a length taller than the rest, the *I* anonymous, simply part of the writing, unemphasized, controlled. Deliberate. She knows the letters bear witness to the early construction of a web into which her mother had been caught, just as Coriola was when she met Fanian at thirty-two and twisted under him, roiled in a lust that surprised her.

In her last home, two words Coriola learned long after

she sits writing to understand, writing to make sense of it to William, whom, in the spring of her fortieth year, she does not yet dare love, words she had not been able to yield to completely, fearing the absolute that made of life an even greater contradiction, nonetheless surfaced and lingered: contra natura, lit by a light that was not reason and that reason would have rejected if Coriola had not been beyond reason in her dying. At forty she pulls on boots, fetches a shopping bag from the hook behind the kitchen door, passes the hallway mirror that casts back her image of herself, and notes only the contradiction: how could the mother who snapped at her ten-year-old daughter for writing a poem laugh at a crush five years later? If her mother had not laughed, if her father had not hurled Desmond across the room, if one of the teachers who turned to Melissa had turned to her instead, if Stephen had liked riding and Peter had come with her, would Coriola have had her rite of passage into sex and love with a large blond riding instructress? If she had not had that initiation, would the sequence have followed that leads her to be standing now, at this moment, at the crossing, waiting for the lights to change, staring at these thoughts while William pushes his way into her mind and her mother's face hovers, permanently present, behind him? If . . . As she is released by the green light into movement, she sees reflected in that small word all the strangeness of life, the possibilities and alternatives that chance events prevent from being realized, the stories that are created, the lives that are lived because one arbitrary moment is added to an arbitrary situation which has itself been fashioned by arbitrary moments and situations linked each to each by chance. If she had not stripped in the greenhouse, her family would not have moved away in an attempt by her father to escape the anger of his guilt. If they had not moved away, she would not have met the riding instructress . . .

Coriola looks at the trees breathing a mist of watery green, knows herself a random accident in an accidental world, and knows even that perception is neither inevitable nor part of any plan. Many have lived and will live without knowing or caring that there is no reason, and many have and will live caring deeply. Neither those who know nor those who do not can do any more than go on living or choose to die, she thinks, waiting in the queue, looking at the pale greenhouse tomatoes, remembering their insipid taste and deciding on a hot vegetable for the meal she will be preparing for William; she thinks that perhaps the choice of death is less arbitrary than the choice to go on living. But when she has paid, placed the brown paper parcel in the shopping bag and left, she wonders why she should have thought that. There is no difference in the arbitrariness of either: it is merely something to do with the tidiness of death. Death is a slut. Life is slovenly.

5

$\mathcal{C}$oriola appeared to absorb her first affair into the fabric of her days. But its dye stained her life a color she might not have chosen had she been given a chance. She might not have chosen to give up riding, in which she was proficient enough for it to be an option, an alternative to a more academic career where she would be unlikely to shine. She could have chosen that smaller pond and been a bigger fish if, within six months of the breakup, an at first imperceptible revulsion had not seeped into her and become so overwhelming she was sick on the side of the road on her way back from the riding lesson, then on her way there, stared at by Tom, a classmate who had taken to accompanying her since he had first noticed the unruly black hair and found himself erect every time he saw her: he wanted to kiss her, but she was so tall he wasn't sure their lips would meet without her stooping to him. And somehow that she should stoop seemed beyond the realms of possibility. The only option was to walk awkwardly by her side and invent ways of making her laugh. Next time, he thought after she had wiped her mouth with a dirty handkerchief he had dug out of the back of his trousers, he'd hold her hand: she was suddenly small and vulnerable, but he didn't like the smell of sick.

When they reached the stables he sauntered back with Kate, who knew how to flirt, and before he knew what had happened he was losing the virginity he had, defiantly, prided himself on wishing to keep until he should find the woman he would love all his life. He had had the contradictory ambition of being a priest, and the revelation of the ruthlessness of sex reinforced the ambition, which also became a protection against the girl and his recurring desire for her. Nonetheless, he continued to accompany Coriola, though not as frequently. He liked her oddness, he told himself when he could not cope with the complexities of wanting two girls at once, at the same time as wishing to dedicate his life to a celibate priesthood.

The smell of horses made Coriola sick, the sight of jodhpured girls and women made her sick, speaking to the riding instructress made her sick, the sight of the tall blond woman made her tingle with what she does not realize until a quarter of a century later is resentment, and she was sick. Again and again she dredged her system until she finally gave in and did not return to the stables.

"What is the matter with you Coriola?"
"Nothing."

"But you're being sick all the time. We should see a doctor."

"If you want."

"I certainly do want."

There is nothing wrong with her that a boyfriend wouldn't put right, the doctor did not say. Instead he said, "She's a big girl."

She was big; the relationship with the riding instructress had allowed her to reach five foot nine without her realizing it. She stood in front of the mirror one day and was astonished at her size. She took off all her clothes and gazed at the reflection. The woman who faced her had nothing to do with her. It was not the obvious signs of womanhood, the breasts and pubic hair, that shocked her: they had been curiosities she had somehow accepted, though she thought it unlikely they were permanent, more likely she would lose them one day as gradually as she had acquired them, and with them the monthly nuisance that never came monthly and always surprised her, staining her clothes at absurd moments and disappearing for weeks and weeks. It was something in the alteration of her figure, the expansion of the hips and the narrowing of the waist, the shape of the legs, the shape of the arms. The way the head stood on the neck, and the neck fanned into the shoulders and merged with the large breasts. The way, under the breasts, the chest flattened and then swelled slightly into the stomach. The way, she thinks at forty, turning around and craning at her back, the way the buttocks expand and fold into the top of the legs. She looked like the riding instructress, she thought at seventeen, and was sick because she could not lie on the floor and beat her legs against the ground and scream that she didn't want it, she didn't want to be like that. She didn't want to be.

"I'm leaving," she told Tom, whose lankiness she liked, whose spots she ignored in favor of the pronounced black eyebrows above dark green eyes, who, without thinking, had taken out a handkerchief and given it to her when she was sick and then had stood, concerned as much as embarrassed. The embarrassment she understood, the concern surprised her.

"Oh,"Tom said. "Where are you going?"

"I'm staying with my grandmother for the summer."

"Oh," Tom said. "Can I write to you?"

"If you want."

"I'm going to be a priest," Tom said, surprising himself. It seemed a peculiarly inappropriate moment to say it.

"Really? Why?"

"I have a vocation."

"Really? What does it feel like?"

"You know you have to do it."

"Really?"

"Yes."

"Can you change your mind?"

"Not if it's a vocation."

"Can you be wrong?"

"You mean think you have a vocation and not have it?"

"Yes."

"I suppose so. I'll be saying mass."

"Oh. Will you write to me?"

"Yes."

"Will you tell me about a vocation?"

She had never in her short life not wanted to be, not even when she lay on the floor in a paroxysm at the age of six. She had never considered her body, not even when Desmond had cupped her breasts, or the riding instructress had searched among the folds for the place that would awaken her senses. Living had been a quite precise expression for what she was and therefore, like her name, not something she dwelled on. But now there was the dislocation, the body did things, became woman, that had nothing to do with her. She was possessed, she thought in the frantic way young people have; she was possessed by her body and could not escape: she remembered the riding instructress, writhing at the touch of her hand, exploding into sighs and moans, and knew herself capable of that. She was sick again.

"Coriola, I'm worried about you. Really worried."

"I'm all right."

"You're not eating."

"I don't want to be sick again."

"I think I'll take you to the doctor."

"I'm all right, Gran, I went. I'm all right, the doctor said."

"You must eat."

"I will."

"Have something now. Bread and butter. Have some cake, I bought it specially."

"Thank you, Gran. Can I have it at dinner?"

"If you promise you'll eat it."

"Promise."

The grandmother was small: Coriola towered over her. Her knees were bad, her eyes were bad, but she strode purposefully with her stick through a wilderness with carefully constructed paths.

"I like the smell of weeds," she told Coriola, leaning on her arm. "Wild flowers are infinitely more lovely than roses." "I climbed on a ladder to kiss him on the day of the wedding," she told her when they looked through the album, and laughed. She was a few years younger than Coriola would be when she was taken to hospital to die and would live a few years longer, dying quietly in her sleep while Coriola fought to die at twenty-two. Coriola looked at the faded picture and smiled.

"You look lovely."

"Oh, yes, I was lovely all right. He was mad for me, he liked me so small. But it was a joke, him so tall and big, the tall and the short of it we were called. Everyone laughed, they dared me, they said to me, 'Come on,' they said, 'let's see you climb the ladder to kiss him.' Well, I did. We cut the cake with me perched on the ladder and him holding me by the waist with one arm so I wouldn't fall."

"Were you happy?"

"Oh, yes."

Coriola knew the story of the ladder: every time she had seen her grandmother, it seemed, the story was repeated, and she had never wondered at her happiness, assuming that the grandmother had not in fact been real. The world had been a set made simply to serve as back-drop to her own, the only life. The grandmother had been merely grandmother and functioned as that: she had no autonomous existence. After their visits to her, she simply disappeared, was no longer there, like a character in a book, and the thank-you letters Coriola had to write, the cards she received were not an indication of a life lived outside her perception but yet another prop to the one life that was really being lived, her own.

When the grandmother told the story of the ladder, it had been just a story, and the notion of real things, like happiness or unhappiness, did not come into it. She wondered suddenly if her grandmother's body was like her own, having until that moment simply assumed there was nothing beyond the particular, sweet-smelling blouses and skirts, long cardigans and heavy dark shoes, having some-how denied flesh to her, having simply, really, not ever thought about it before; and she was sick again, but se-cretly, late at night, when the grandmother was asleep.

She did not seek to know more of her grandmother's life, but not, now, because she knew there was nothing more, but because to open up a life to her gaze would mean standing the world on its head, would mean know-ing herself as another example of a kind. She would have to align herself side by side with her grandmother, her mother, the riding instructress, and define herself as one of those, just as, in their walks through the garden and the fields beyond, the grandmother would point her stick and say, "That's pheasant's eye, that's milkwort," until Coriola could not not know that among the mass of green and wild flowers there was columbine, larkspur, dame's violet, dusky cranesbill.

At forty-one, pregnant with her only child, she searches obsessively for the lost album, she rakes through her brain for information about her grandmother and about the grandfather who had died without Coriola noticing, shrinking from an imposing six foot something . . .

"How tall was Grandad, Mum?" she asks her mother, who gazes past her at the bare trees framed by the window in the hospice.

"My father?"

Coriola holds her breath, hesitates. "No, Dad's father."

"Oh. He was well over six foot four when he was young."

"You don't know exactly?"

"I can't remember. Never saw such a transformation as before he died, and in such a short time."

Coriola knows the euphemism of the phrase, watching the transformation in her tall mother, shrunk to the proportions of her grandmother by the illness.

"And your father? Tell me about your father."

"What is there to tell?"

"There are no photographs, there is nothing. When did he die?"

"I wasn't married."

"What was he like?"

"What was he like?" Her mother turns shrunken features to Coriola.

"Don't you remember?"

"I don't remember." She turns her head away.

"We've never talked of your family. We never saw them."

"No."

"Your mother, tell me about your mother."

"She was ill, she died." Coriola's mother closes her eyes.

"And your brothers—why did we never see them? Did you quarrel?"

The mother opens her eyes, suddenly alert. She looks at Coriola, whose heart beats as if she were performing a crime, invading the tacit territory of her mother's past that had never been spoken about, of which there had seemed to be, there was perhaps nothing to know.

"I'm tired, Coriola. I'll sleep."

The mother turns slowly, painfully on her side, closes her eyes.

"I'll sit by you for a while."

"Thank you."

And walking away from the hospice, she cries not for her, dwindling certainly towards death, but at the loss of the exact height of her grandfather: there is no one she can ask, every one of her father's large family has died, killed in random ways at random times. Some here, some there. Her father, the youngest, died sliced by the vehicle he had been driving on what, he told his wife before he went, would be one of his last business trips, the year Coriola was offered her first important part, as Portia, the year before she met Fanian. He was tired, the father told the mother, of hotel rooms and suitcases. He would go to the end of the year and retire, early but not too early. They would potter around, slow down their lives to the rhythm of the seasons and the pace of the day. Maybe they would discover ways of loving each other, he thought in the car, flashing the light to overtake.

There is no one who had known her grandfather; her brothers remember less than she does. The grandparents revert to being story, standing, the tall and the short of it, permanently kissing, she perched on the stepladder, he beside her, holding her small waist: what did it feel like looking down on the face of the woman who was to be her grandmother? Were her arms around his neck the next minute, after the click of the camera? Had she taken his face in her hands? Did the mustache tickle her lips?

And if her father's mother's life is merely picture, frozen and still, what of her mother's family? Coriola tosses in bed that night, unable to turn away from the white, the blank, the darkness of a past that cannot be known. All gone, not even a snapshot to bring them back, resurrect them in the memory. She feels incapable of inventing her mother's past, the two brothers, the mother who suckled her as she in turn suckled Coriola, the father who stood outside the door—how tall, how broad? Coriola knows nothing, and her mother will not remember and yield her story.

"There must have been something. Mum, can't you tell me? Why did you quarrel?"

"All this time and it's still why why why. Hush, Coriola, what does it matter?"

"Let's give our child a past crowded with incident," she tells the absent William as dawn slices its light through the curtains. "Let's fill her days with pictures and memories to latch her to the earth, tie her, bind her to the earth. Even if it's all lies, what does it matter, if they make her sure of the future because of a past?"

At seventy-five, one of the few vivid memories, etched with a brightness that came from nowhere and had no shadows, was of her grandmother, small and fierce, pointing at the wilderness with her stick and her voice, distinctive through all the years, unlike any other voice, saying, "Wild flowers are infinitely more lovely than roses."

In the long meditation of a slow dying, it came to her with the power of a vision, and she lay, when it faded, content.

6

She was sick again.

"Coriola, I'm worried about you. Really worried."

"I'm all right, Dad."

"You're not eating."

"I don't want to be sick."

"I think we'll take you to another doctor."

"I'm all right, Mum. Stop fussing."

"You never go out. You should go out and make friends."

Coriola shrugged: Tom had left, suddenly, before Coriola returned. He had written to her once, and then a letter waited for her to say he was off to be a priest. He was brokenhearted, he did not tell her, Kate had got bored with him and, frightened by the violence of jealousy at seeing her on the back of a motorbike on the way from the stables, he fled into the arms of his vocation. He would make a good priest, and when Coriola saw him again, bumped into him on the train after her affair with Fanian had wrung from her any vestige of hope, he would offer her another, cleaner handkerchief with which to dry her tears, and absent himself for a further twenty years.

"Isn't there anyone in your class you like?" her father asked. "I'm worried, Coriola. Can't you try to make friends? What happened to Jane?"

Jane bought pink sweaters and at that very moment was allowing the hand of a presentable young man to move gradually farther up her leg until it touched the cotton pants and Jane's legs opened.

Almost a moment passed before she could muster the will to close them, to remove the eager fingers. If she had been Coriola, she would have said that pressing the legs together at that moment had been a Herculean task, she would have wondered why she had been incapable of not opening them in the first place and been astonished at the power of sex. Jane took that for granted, her relationship with her body was much more straightforward, it did not need analysis. She was therefore free to concentrate on other things: she closed her legs, smoothed down the skirt, allowed the hand to rest on her breast, under the pink sweater, to rub the pointed, erect nipples, but not below the waist, no, because she did not want to be thought fast.

Coriola on her forty-first birthday, her legs and heart wide open to William who enters her, thrusting and pushing through the past to the present, ready to take her into the future before leaving her, at fifty-eight, to make of their past yet another future, Coriola looks back at her ignorance at eighteen: you lived on cloud nine. Why had such realities simply not been real for her? She had no notion of what being fast meant. When such things were discussed among her classmates, where was she?

Coriola and Jane had made friends because Jane fancied Stephen, Coriola's younger brother, who, flattered by the attention of an older girl, bragged about how far they'd gone to half his class. As a result, he failed to lose his virginity in her, and Coriola lost a precarious friendship that would have taught her as much as her friendship with Melissa would have if Melissa had not moved out of her life at ten; Melissa, who by the age of twenty was to receive and give pleasure to half a dozen men, and by the time she was twenty-four was living with a man she was not ready to marry, though he bullied and coaxed, wanting to settle down, wanting to be sure of her.

"Why, it's perfectly all right as it is. Why marry?"

"You don't love me."

There was some truth in that, Melissa acknowledged somewhere deep within herself; but out loud she protested that of course she did, she wouldn't be with him, would she, if she didn't. And he went to the office shaking with a rage he could not show and did not know was simply a result of not being able to control things, to have them the way he would have liked them. He threw himself into his work, rising quickly despite his youth, and within a year, when Coriola moved to town in search of work, he had split up with Melissa and gratefully taken a young girl who did not know her mind or her heart to his heart and to the altar in a flurry of bridesmaids and proud parents. Melissa, who had known so clearly she did not want to marry him, although she had always added a precautionary "yet," thought herself heartbroken and was in fact confused. It had seemed so simple and inevitable to give her body and receive another body's pleasure. But to give her life, her days, her time to another when there was so much to do and so many others to love? It was absurd. As Coriola at twenty-five hunted for work and found her first job in a seedy pub, doing a striptease on Saturday nights, Melissa went back to school, determined to give herself the chance she had let slip at sixteen, when boys and sex had seemed the only important thing.

At twenty, however, Coriola was in the hospital, dying of starvation.

_T_hrough the seesaw years that followed the force-feeding days, Coriola, incapable of engaging in the basic activity to maintain her body in life, returned and left the hospital, returned and left the hospital. Incapable of appreciating the patience of others, she emptied herself, taking the shape of a slave; looked at herself in mirrors and saw only flesh; tossed and turned in her bed to find ways to acquire fleshlessness and live. She fought with cunning all who sought to subvert reality as she saw it and give her illusion.

"You will die if you go on like this."

"How can we convince you that you are skin and bone?"

"Look, look at yourself. Just look, can't you?"

Sometimes, late at night, weary with gnawing cold, weary with permanent unacknowledged hunger, weary of the ache of bone and nerve in constant contact, weary with the exhaustion of those whose perceptions differ from the norm, she cried and wished she could visit the mirror and that it would show her what others saw. And she would rise, she would go, skeletal and hairy, and stand in the dark, willing the mirror to conform to others' way of seeing, that she may yield and become flesh once more. And she would switch on the light abruptly, hoping to surprise the reflection into showing some different image. And she saw the large, full body of a woman, breasts ready for sucking and suckling, strong legs to clinch the body of a man into her, a belly eager to carry seeds of new flesh that would be born in the likeness of man, in her likeness. And she would pull on clothes, creep downstairs and out into the pouring rain, in the mild night damp, under a blazing starlit sky, and run so that she might no longer have flesh; and be in the hospital a few days later, bewildered by tubes and words and the strong insistent voices.

"You will die if you go on like this."

"How can I convince you you are a walking skeleton?"

"Look, look, for Christ's sake, can't you see?"

She couldn't see it as they saw it. She couldn't. They must be conspiring against her, all in unison wanting her to be gross so that they might laugh at the monster they had fashioned, at the power of their persuasion. Look, she imagined them telling each other, whispering in white coats, behind screens, look how easy it is to convince someone of what is not true: she now believes that she is no longer fat; we have convinced her. She now looks in mirrors and sees slimness where there is fat. Look what we can do. Let us move on to greater things, become conquerors in a world that has no certainties, now we have experimented with this child's perception and she believes herself other than she is. We can take over the world by persuasion, by insisting that their perceptions are the illusions of sick minds, that what they see is not what they see, but what we see. And they would laugh long whispered laughs, pulling the screen across, unbut toning white coats, their naked hanging stomachs shaking with laughter, faces hidden by the gauze that decked the hospital of her dreams like streamers.

"You will die."

"Can't you see you're starving yourself to death?"

She did not want to die. She did want to die. She did not know what she wanted. She wanted to live and not be flesh. She did not like things as they were, and could not lie and beat her legs on the ground, so she escaped and emptied herself of the food being pumped into her bloodstream.

"You are sick, my darling girl, please see that."

"You are ill, but we can put that right, just trust us, will you?"

Oh, but she wouldn't. She trusted no one. How dare they give her flesh? She knew what they were about. How dare they torture her so? And the sequence continued, tedious and relentless. She would eat a little more, be sent home and eat a little less, return and eat a little more. A child of her age, Coriola at forty, on a warm August day, fighting off wasps and flies in the small garden she and her mother have let go to seed, probes for explanations. There must have been some psychological reason, she thinks, she writes, she eventually tells William—the riding instructress, the boy who had not kissed her, the confusion of pretty Melissa and Desmond cupping her breast, being swiped by a blow; the father strict in his own fear, the mother attentive to the brothers, unable to obliterate the scar of her first resentment; Stephen suddenly a boy with hair, walking naked and shameless to the bathroom opposite her, occasionally erect and leering, though not at her but at magazines she sneaked into their room and looked through, women like the riding instructress in black and red, exposing pudenda, opening it with provocative fingers, barely covered buttocks jutting out as girls knelt on all fours and turned, looking at her straight in the eye, inviting. Was it fear of sex? Was it apprehension of choices before her, Coriola on the brink of adulthood not knowing that adulthood is merely one day after another, not some momentous transformation? The parents insisting when she felt the weight of her ignorance like a mountain pressing in on her, but under which she could not hide; knowing all these years she had bluffed and one day she would be found out, fingers would point at her and eyebrows would lift, and she would be as naked, as exposed as those girls in magazines, but powerless.

And Coriola, walking to the hospice in the long summer afternoon, wonders, astounded at the tenacity of the body that had fought as her mother's was fighting; that despite everything had not died; that had, in the end, won its right to live and lord it over her until she had had to yield, to compromise and accept its half of the inheritance that is existence. Though that, mused Coriola at seventy-five, curled on her side on the bed suddenly too large for her shrinking frame, that is a division into body

and soul that no more reflects reality than the ravings of
a young anorectic. And yet what does reflect reality? Was
there not, even, some truth in the ravings of Coriola at
twenty-two? As much truth as there is in the philosophical
division of body and soul that shaped the world for cen-
turies? Had not the same distinction been the cause of
Coriola's illness? Had not Coriola sought to do what men
in all ages and in all places where body and soul are placed
in adversary roles have sought to do, to obliterate the one
and cultivate the other? Martyrs and hermits, fakirs and
stylites, ascetics and flagellants all punished the body in
an effort to refashion the world into a construct without
chance and decay, without change and death? Could it
have been the very terror of death that drove Coriola so
close to it at twenty-two, Coriola wonders at forty, changing the angle of the pillow as her mother changes position,
lies for a while on her back, talking in incomprehensible
short bursts.

"Throw it away," she says suddenly, turning her eyes
from the tree.

"What?"

"The key," she says, closing her eyes, sinking back
into the pillow that holds her almost sitting in the white
bed.

Is the reality of death not psychological enough? Not
the foundation of all possible psychological explanation?
The terror of not having existed, suddenly existing, in a
moment becoming mere yellow parchment on a white
bed? The terror of it, Coriola thinks, no closer to death
than at twenty-two, leaving her mother in a pool of light,
curled up on her side, watching the game of leaves and

light played by the trees that encircle and protect the hospice. How can anyone sustain the thought of it? Must it not be buried under an avalanche of sand and words? Or be tamed by playing games with it? Had not Coriola in all misery been merely playing, playing to tame death?

8

*A*t seventy-five, wizened and cancer-ridden, Coriola looked and saw the mysterious necessity of it and smiled through the terror, ready to relinquish herself to dust.

"Mummy," Coriola's daughter said, "Mummy, you don't have to be in the hospital, you could come home with us."

And would her friend, the orderly who came and sat with her, would he come and sit by her in a room in her daughter's house? And the visitors who came to the other beds and sometimes waved at her or came up and said hello? There was a stranger next to her daughter who, Coriola knew, was her husband, though they had not married as Coriola's grandmother and grandfather had married, she perched on a stepladder wearing lace, turning up her face to his kiss, or as she marries William, quietly in a registry office after her mother's death, not long before her daughter is born. Or indeed as her mother married her father, Coriola imagines at forty, in virginal white and top hat, walking out of the church under a shower of confetti. Her daughter was small, like Coriola's grandmother: the man towered over her, and her belly was large with the child she was carrying. Coriola wanted to ask the man's name but knew she should know. Looking at the way he turned towards her daughter, she thought it was William suddenly, though he had a mustache. He had the doctor's grey eyes, William's grey eyes. Her daughter's father's grey eyes.

"What color were Dad's eyes?" She could not remember. She thought they had been light. She could not remember the color of her own eyes, or her mother's. She hoped her daughter's husband did not slide his eyes away, and that she would live to see the child born.

At seventy-five she was able to say, not by looking into a mirror do you see straight but by obliquity, and remembered the confused child with greater affection than the adult who sought to define, and by seeking to define, reduced necessity to determinism, mystery to psychology, life to existence, reality to rationality: there must be a rational explanation, that is the chorus of the new enlightenment, haunting us into despair, Coriola thought, lying on her deathbed, conquered by life into submission. And we miss the light, dancing through the leaves of the plane tree opposite the window, transforming glass into crystal, crystal into prism and rainbow; and the daffodils stubbornly giving themselves to whoever may take pleasure in looking, giving themselves regardless of whether there is anyone who will take pleasure in looking. She was aware, in the silence, of a concertina in time, of the clashing of plaintive sounds as past, present and future meshed into end and beginning, and love, she sighed, imagining her small daughter walking down the ward bearing her child like a trophy—love is the air, contained and unseen, against which the instrument vibrates and makes sound.

One early morning in summer, running away from the sun, Coriola at twenty-four came upon the imprint of a gesticulating skeleton stretched ahead of her. She stopped in her run and the shadow stared up at her in the black silence of fact. Coriola turned this way and that, that it might conform to the reflection she knew. But the imprint insisted, remained as inescapable as its contradictory image. Of course, Coriola argued as she turned to walk slowly home with the shadow at her heels, shadows are always elongated. That's what it is, a trick of the light. See, she told herself, looking at the early morning shadow of trees on the grass and of buildings on the pavement. See how different they are from the objects themselves. But she had never felt such weariness.

She reassured herself that the mirror spoke true, lay on the bed and drifted in and out of a dream, unsure whether it was memory: her brother Peter, whose existence she had forgotten, stood holding a kite as large as himself, staring up at her father who was speaking, but whose words were muffled by the food he was chewing. Coriola watched him take a bite from a bar of chocolate and pass the bar to her. As she took it and brought it to her mouth, hunger surged through her crotch to her belly, passed her belly to her head and feet like the orgasm she had never experienced, warm, like the sudden hot towel wrapped around her as a child being lifted from the bath and set on her mother's lap, towel and arms enveloping her completely.

Like an orgasm, it left her weak on the bed, aware of the breeze through a blue sky carrying unseen kites held by unknown children, aware of the sun blessing objects with shadows, the silence painfully interrupted by the joy of birds. She was alone in the house and would eat. She would eat outside, in the green sunshine. She would perch on the wall that had been host to squirrels and foxes come to drink from the pond her father had built and share bread with fish darting red-green in the water.

"I will eat." Coriola spoke aloud, strange new tears tickling her temple and the arch of her nose before sinking into the pillow. "I will eat, I will."

She rose, shuffled out of her room, down the stairs and into the kitchen.

"I will eat bread. And cheese. I will eat biscuits. I will eat slowly."

She spoke to the light that poured through the window, to the silence of the house at rest, to the absent mother who had stood by and had somehow succeeded in not allowing the dislike she felt for her daughter to take over from the anguish of watching a creature trapped by its own perceptions; who, like her father, had been surprised by the inescapable nature of parenthood that sent them both out in search of ways, doctors, treatments to prevent her death.

"What did we do?"

"Was it, is it, our fault?"

"It's my fault."

The inescapable ingredient of parental love: guilt. Guilt at being too human for the ambition, the certainty, the desire that the child will be a perfect creature in a perfect world. And watch the dream disintegrate, in the first loss of temper—she's so bad-tempered, I don't know what's got into her, has a tantrum practically every day, is going through a difficult phase, is a devil—in the first signs of a flaw parallel, identical to the parent's—she has my stubbornness, my wildness, my—and see the illusion momentarily reassert itself when the child sleeps or clambers into your lap and lies sucking its thumb, looking out at the world with an intensity of stillness that cannot last. Guilt at not liking your child, so like you, yet loving her. It may not even be a question of love, Coriola thinks at forty; whatever that word may mean, she writes in February, before it becomes so clear there is no longer any need to express or explain, before her mother begins the long journey to death, before she meets William and in early autumn feels the first swelling of the breasts, the first alterations in her pregnant body. It may simply be the identification of one who will one day be dying with the other who is already enduring; or an instinct of responsibility, the necessity to do something, and what else can one do but love the dying? Coriola, a few months later, sitting by her mother's side, knows the responsibility is not cause but effect. Her mother can hardly lift her hand from the coverlet most of the time. But sometimes Coriola visits her and she is sitting up, reading, having combed her hair and daubed lipstick on ashen lips, and Coriola must hide the tenderness that would make her take her mother in her arms and rock her, such a small, such a puny, such a hopeless gesture—Mother, Mother, don't die, don't become smaller, don't. Don't leave me with the responsibility of your death, of never again not knowing that death is inescapable.

But at twenty-four she spoke to Peter, whose existence she had just remembered, who had stared at her, puzzled and irritated, angry and resentful at the attention being drawn away from the problems of his adolescence, occasionally moved by the dullness of her look, the pallor of her face, the emptiness in the eyes he had always liked looking at before, when Coriola had been Coriola who bossed and gave him treats, who had taken him to the park to fly kites and sail boats when he was little. She spoke to Stephen with whom she had long ago stopped quarreling because she needed all her energy to live flesh-less and joust with death, who had gone away without her noticing and was now in another town, the town to which the riding instructress had moved with her lover and Rita, the girl-child who rushed across the playground, brown-red hair bouncing on round cheeks, not yet puzzled by two mothers and no father; the town where Melissa was living with the man she was not ready to marry, who would leave her in a few weeks to marry the girl he had met at the office Christmas party, paler, taller than Melissa, more angular. But a good girl, just the kind of wife he needed, he reminded himself when his eyes strayed towards red-haired women at the parties they went to, at the dinners she hosted through the years. Just the right kind of mother, he thought with satisfaction, watching his son and daughter grow, at the breakfast table, rarely in the evening. The kind of woman he could not feel guilty about betraying, sex had been so irrelevant to the creation of a family whose picture could be on the desk, next to the internal phone, placed so that clients and visitors could see it more clearly than he.

"Where is everyone?" Coriola asked the light. But she was glad to be alone to take her first steps. She would eat slowly, she repeated to herself, afraid of the nausea that stalked behind her determination. "I will not be sick. I will eat slowly, just a little bread and a little cheese. Then I will rest. And I will eat again."

Perhaps they had all left her? she wondered as she opened the fridge, comforted by its hum. She looked at the cheese and fought the revulsion. "I will eat it. I will go out in the garden and eat it with bread. With bread and butter I will eat it."

And some days later, as she struggled to keep food down that surged into her mouth—her body a mercenary torturer ready to switch and fight on the side of death now that she had conceded victory—she entered a shop at a particular angle, so that her reflection in glass was itself reflected in a mirror: though the glass showed an image of herself she had created, overblown, bursting with flesh, the mirror suddenly refused to conspire, and Coriola saw the face of the wizened old woman she was to become at seventy-five, dying in a white hospital room with rattling metal cabinets. The old woman, wearing the black clothes of winter and mourning, stared sideways but through her from sockets too deep for eyes. It was over almost before Coriola had taken the next step and changed the angle so completely she was not able to repeat it: she walked out and in again and saw only the familiar reflection.

She returned to the shop whenever her will buckled under the weight of effort and the persistent image in the mirror that became even more swollen and bloated, and though the vision never recurred, other things came to the surface unbidden, as if her mind had stored them for just such an emergency.

"Nonsense," her dead grandmother's brisk voice said. "You shouldn't lose any more weight. You're just a big tall girl, you need to be well covered. You don't want to be a scarecrow, do you?"

A doctor, whose eyelids drooped wearily at the corner, but whose eyes had steeled themselves, grey and strong, into hers: "Why should we lie?"

"I don't know. Why don't I see it your way?"

"You're not looking, you're imagining."

"No."

"Look at me, Coriola. Don't slide your eyes away."

"I'm not sliding my eyes away."

"Look at me."

"All right."

"Coriola, I am not lying. None of us is lying. You are lying to yourself."

"Why should I lie to myself?"

"I don't know. And I don't care. I just want you to stop, now, this minute."

"How can I when I am not?"

"Can't you trust me?"

"No."

And the eyelids drooped farther, but the eyes did not turn away; they looked straight, challenging.

"Remember, Coriola, I am not lying."

"What was the name of that doctor?"

The mother turned to Coriola, surprised by her words, unused to being addressed by a daughter who for seven years had belonged to demons created by mirrors and perceptions.

"He had grey eyes."

"You noticed his eyes?"

"I remember his eyes."

"Darling, I can't possibly remember. We've been to so many doctors."

"I'm sorry."

Coriola remembered the look on her mother's face most clearly at seventy-five, though at forty she recognizes it when she opens the door of her room at the hospice after William and she have been away for a week, and her mother turns. Her features are transformed by it, and Coriola at twenty-four saw that indeed she was ill.

"Can we find out, please, Mum?"

"Find out?"

"Who the doctor was?"

"Yes, of course, if . . ."

"Thanks."

It became a parallel search: at the same time as Coriola sought her body, she searched for the man who had looked her straight in the eye and said he was not lying, that she was. She told herself each day that if she ate, if she ate the portion of rice—not too much and then I'll eat it—if she ate the portion of meat, the potatoes, the vegetables in butter, the cream, they would find him.

"I wish I could remember his name."

"Do you remember how many times you saw him?"

"No. I'm ill, aren't I, Mum?"

"Yes."

"What is it?"

"Anorexia."

It did not help to know. Only the doctor would be able to explain why for seven years she had fought so hard against her body.

"You do look better."

"Thank you."

It wasn't he.

"Well, it's nice to see you again. You've put on some weight."

Coriola fought the nausea at the phrase. It wasn't he.

"You're on course. You'll be all right. Just keep eating, won't you?"

Nor he. She shivered, tempted to retreat, to stop fighting.

But he rose from his chair, came around the desk, walked towards her, shook her skeletal hand.

"Do sit down."

And he looked at her straight in the eye, smiling.

"Welcome to the human race."

"Am I lying to myself?"

"You were."

"Why?"

"You're afraid. But I don't know of what. We can try and find out if you want."

"I want to see what you see."

"We are all afraid, Coriola. You will never see what I see, just as I never see what anyone else sees. We're alone."

"But—"

"You've just fought harder than most against knowing that. And the fighting has isolated you even more."

"What shall I do?"

"Eat and live."

"Why?"

He looked at her and smiled. The eyelids drooped, the eyes lit up.

"Because you want to."

And Coriola smiled too.

"As simple as that?"

"I think so."

"Mum, hug me."

"Coriola, don't cry."

"Hug me, Mum, hug me."

"How old are you?"

"Forty-five."

"That's ancient."

"Isn't it?"

"Can I kiss you?"

"When you're ten pounds fatter."

"I'm afraid."

"I know."

"I think I'm in love with you."

"You'll get over it."

"Can we kiss?"

"When you're fatter."

"Can you hold my hand?"

"It's not simple."

"No, of course not."

"I don't like loving you. It hurts. And you don't love me."

"I'm an old married man."

"Can I touch your eyes?"

"No, I don't think so, Coriola."

"Dad, hold me, hold me. Dad."

"Hold my hand, Dad. Stay with me."

"How many children do you have?"

"Three, a girl and two boys."

"You're just a little younger than my father."

"If I'd married at twenty instead of thirty, I could have a daughter your age."

"Is your daughter pretty?"

"She's fifteen and lovely."

"I was horrible at fifteen."

"Everyone at fifteen thinks they're horrible. Twenty years on they realize . . ."

"So we're not to kiss?"

"You knew that all along."

They looked at each other.

"Yes, I think I did."

"You're very sound in some ways you know."

"But not in others."

"No, not in others. No one is."

"No consolation, of course."

"No consolation at all."

"Is your wife pretty?"

"Not as good-looking as you'll be."

"Really?"

"Really. Just a few more pounds."

"I wish I could see it as you do."

"What?"

"I looked at myself in the mirror, and you said I'm good-looking. I don't see it."

"Keep looking."

"Are we flirting?"

"Not yet."

"What's the difference?"

"You're asking me."

"Let's go to see a film, come on, Peter, let's go."

"Why are you being nice to me?"

"I'm not sure. I want you to be happy."

"I want to touch you."

"You won't always be able to say that safely you know."

"I'm afraid."

"We're all in the same boat."

"That doesn't help in the slightest."

"I know. But you must make do with what I can do."

"What shall I do when I'm fat and healthy?"

"Don't get fat. But stay healthy."

"Yes, but what shall I do?"

"Live."

"I have to do something, haven't I?"

"Live."

"You're no help anymore."

"Good, it means you're all right."

"Can't you tell me what to do?"

"No."

"Why?"

"Because you have to find that out for yourself."

"I don't know, I don't want to do anything."

"Then don't."

"And how do I live?"

"You'll live."

"Will I be a well-adjusted member of the human race?"

"All signs point in that direction."

"Will I lose anything?"

"Probably."

"Is it worth it?"

"I don't know. You ask too many questions."

"What can I do to stop?"

"I don't know."

"If only there were a few answers."

"There are. But they're not words."

Yes, she thought, he's right. His eyes are an answer.
He has not slid his eyes away, not even once.

* * *

"I'm going to be a belly dancer."

"You do that—very healthy. You use all the muscles."

"Doctor, be serious. What shall I do?"

"All right, I'll be serious." He leaned forward on his chair, brought his hands together on the desk and looked at Coriola. "What do you want to do?"

"I don't know, I keep telling you," Coriola screamed.

The doctor smiled. "But you do, you're just afraid of saying it. Coriola, don't slide your eyes away."

"No, all right."

They looked at each other and smiled.

"Why is it so difficult?"

"Don't ask why."

"All things to all men."

"A whore?"

Coriola laughed, throwing back her head, abandoning herself to it with the lost delight of the ten-year-old rolling on the floor next to Melissa. The doctor relaxed in his chair and looked at her, smiling.

"I want to be an actress."

"Well, I was nearly right."

Coriola giggled. "Maybe I'll do both."

"No, don't be a whore. But tenderness is never wasted."

And how wrong he was, Coriola thinks at forty. How much tenderness has been wasted, she thinks, lying under the thirty-year-old son of the doctor who saved her at twenty-four—William, whose eyes are shut, whose face is closed and absorbed though not distant.

9

Within a year of the vision of contradictory images cast back by two reflections, Coriola's body was healed of starvation: enough flesh hid the awkward projection of bone in knees and elbows; her shoulders and neck were covered by a layer that glowed under the skin; soft down replaced the long hairs on the arms. Curves replaced angularity, and Coriola felt better. It was as if her sight had improved, as if she had emerged after walking for years in a veiled landscape. She could stand in front of the mirror and look at herself without horror. At least, she told the doctor on one of the last occasions, she knew she might feel horror and prepared herself. But she was not comfortable: "Somehow it just doesn't fit."

"It will take a long time. You have worked so hard to destroy your body, it will be a long time before you can become part of its sensations once more. But you will.

Don't worry. You're beautiful," he said, shaking her hand, laughing with his eyes.

Is this beauty, she wondered, looking at herself. She did not believe him, she trusted him but he was wrong. What, where was beauty in the features she learned one by one, the grey eyes set too wide apart, the thin nose that was always a little intrusive, the sharply edged lips, the thick eyebrows, the long neck, the long arms, wide shoulders, the breasts that had remained shrunken, small? She lifted her arms and looked at the black hairs pointing like arrows to the hair at the division of the thighs. If the doctor had seen her as she was now, standing naked in front of the mirror, would he have called her beautiful? She could not believe it.

When she went for her interview at the bar, they almost did not take her because of her breasts. She performed in front of the owner, two barmen and the accountant who had suggested the bar should become a club—they might lose the women, but they'd gain all the workmen within miles, and never mind if the beer was doctored. They took her as much for the eroticism of her uncomprehending face as for the pay she was willing to accept and the fact that the three other girls who had turned up could not move unselfconsciously enough to draw attention away from the dimples of fat on the thighs and the stretch marks around the stomach.

"She appears not to know how obscene she is being. Doesn't look at anyone, as if she's worshipping at some altar only she can see. Very sexy," one of the barmen said as they congratulated each other after her first performance. Coriola lost her virginity to him, hard against the wall of the back entrance to the club. She hardly sighed, though she loved his smile.

"Be happy," the doctor had told her.

She discovered the pleasure of being held by a man and hardly realized how momentous it was: had the riding instructress discovered it, she would not have stood, at the precise moment when the barman put his arms around Coriola and Coriola leaned her head against his chest with the image of the doctor in her mind, and behind it some faded memory of another chest against which a child, sucking its thumb, had lain its head, breathing in the smell of pipe tobacco in rhythm to the lifting and lowering—and felt, for an instant, as if the moment contained, fragmented, slight, like a breath of summer wind, some unspoken answer to a question she did not know she needed to ask. Had the riding instructress discovered it, she would not have stood, having put Rita to bed, anxiously by the drawn curtains waiting for her lover to return, half fearful that she might have met a man at the conference she had gone to.

"Be happy," the doctor had told Coriola.

At forty-one, while the first lilac opens to scent the air, and Coriola lies exhausted with a newborn made by her body groping towards breasts restored to suckling size, she knows happiness resides in the body and wonders why she might have had to undergo and submit to such unhappiness: what had there been in the child who had hurled herself into life with the exuberance of a day drenched in sparkling sunlight that became maimed with unhappiness like a debilitating illness? That made life muffled, somehow distant, permanently distorted in some pervasive but indefinable way, as if between her and it there was some kind of slightly warped glass? It was a flatness of spirit, not an unhappiness that made her cry, though she had felt that too: when the first man, whose smile she had loved, whose heartbeat had been a discovery, left her after a few weeks—"I don't know why, love. It just isn't right," he said; when the second man went after a few days, depriving her of his strong hands—"You're a bit weird, ain't ya?"—when the third man, whose back she clung to, left her several months later, a couple of weeks before she returned to celebrate Stephen's wedding to Susan, a gentle girl who masked her stammer with a blush that heightened the luminosity of her green eyes and brought out auburn highlights in her hair and bore a daughter, Ann, six months after the wedding. Stephen had met her eighteen months before and never tired of looking at her, though she was not beautiful. Coriola, who liked her, found the plumpness of her figure disturbing. It lingered as a trace of nausea that persisted during rehearsals for the first play in which she played the main part, that of a widow bent on marrying her pretty teenage daughter off to a rich neighbor who she knew was homosexual, though the daughter, in the fashion of the time, hardly knew there was anything except the coupling of man and woman and thought that marriage was an economic arrangement, never suspecting a sharing of beds and an involvement of bodies, and was merely puzzled by the effect on her if the hero looked into her eyes.

Coriola had an affair with the actor who played the hero and was puzzled by the lack of effect if he looked into her eyes, or his hands wandered the length and breadth of her body: it was as if there were a thin plastic layer between her skin and any sensation she might have. She felt no revulsion at being touched: she felt nothing, and when the affair ended with the run—"Perhaps you're frigid," he told her when she tried to explain, dismissing her with a shrug, uninterested—she spent two erratic years playing small roles on stages all over the country, in and out of men's beds, loving a different fragment of their bodies, pouring out a tenderness that was not wanted on the same fragment of each man. She did not understand her own desirability, though she could see it in the dimly lit, crowded bar as her body cast suggestive shadows over the upturned faces. They looked at her moving to music, taking off this item of clothing to cover another part of her body with it, swaying along the length of the platform above them, out of reach so they could glimpse the parting of the thighs, the place every one of them wanted to reach.

So strangely desirable, she thought when in the small hours of the morning she made her way back to the bed-sitting room and in the long afternoons replayed to the mirror the teases of strip, incapable of seeing anything but an arrangement of limbs with a particular structure and form that had nothing of what she considered desirability: desirability lay for her, suddenly and forcefully, in shoulders clothed in jackets, in a muscular hand, in the roughness of an unshaven cheek against her breast, in the thick hair on muscled legs and between, where the cock she had first glimpsed erect and manly on her brother crossing the passage to the bathroom overwhelmed her with tenderness each time. Until the brutality of a number of her lovers to whom she had given what the doctor had rejected three, almost four years before, she thought at twenty-eight, still in love with him though she had not seen him—until the dozen men who entered her and left her made her realize an infinite complexity in the workings of the body. Conscious of how the fragments she loved echoed physical features of the doctor, she suspected that all other bodies were substitutes for him to whom she could not give, who had given her a life from which she could no longer turn away. She wrote to him: "I'm so unhappy and I know we could be happy; come to me, let me come to you. Let us be together just once. I'm so unhappy. Think of it as therapy. Let me love you once, only once. If you could love me, I would understand. You said I was beautiful. You told me to be happy. I can't be happy without you. Come to me." She knew he would not reply.

"You're on your own after this session," he had told her. "You must not think of me, but go out and meet someone who can give you what I cannot. Relax, let yourself be loved," he had said.

Because she didn't understand, she thinks at forty-one, putting streamers on the small, on the last Christmas tree on the cabinet by her mother, who looks at her through veiled eyes that occasionally sharpen into awareness and knowledge—"Promise," she says, "the key." She closes her eyes. "Draw the curtain"—because she didn't understand, she was totally uninhibited, successful and unhappy. Her body was a puppet she handled, sprawling its legs, wriggling its hips, covering its breasts with hands, uncovering one without revealing the nipple, for it was the nipple that sent a murmur of sighs and whistles rippling through the dark.

"Come on, show them to us."

"Let's see them move."

She looked past the audience and covered herself, turned her back, bent over to pick up the thin, almost transparent scarf.

"Let's see the cunt, open the legs," the man at the back shouted, his voice breaking like a teenager's.

And Coriola hid and revealed, because that was what they wanted, though for her to show or not was the same. It was nothing more than another feature of her flesh, the mystery lay not in it, but in the effect it had. Did they feel for it what she felt for the rising cock. It seemed inconceivable: never would she want a man to parade in front of her more or less clothed. What she felt for a man's body was a suffocating tenderness, of which a large element was an awareness of deception, as if her body were promising more than it could deliver, and every time a man spilled himself in her, she was conning him into giving her something, his seed, by the illusion that she had something to give him. But there was nothing. It was the knowledge of the nothing she could give that made her tight-chested and ready.

Was it also this knowledge, she wonders at forty-one, that closed her sprawling body from further sensation? Or was it the discrepancy between her desire to reach out to the skin of the doctor whom she had never touched and the relentless attempts to penetrate her? There seemed no connection between the tenderness she felt and the urgent, panting, groaning eagerness to enter her; then to turn away. As if, triumphant, they could dismiss her. Dismiss her because they had entered her. And each time they received nothing from her. Was it her lack of love that prevented it from being anything but a rough violation of bodies? Theirs as well as hers. And perhaps she was most to blame, who could not believe they sought love in a penetration of her body so devoid of tenderness. What did they seek? What did she seek by giving herself without yielding?

At forty she still knows only that she hungers for the anchor the warmth of a body provides: is William's desire parallel, is the energy of his lovemaking nothing less than an expression of warmth given and sought, she wonders, lying under him as the long winter gives way to spring. Her eyes, which had remained open in anticipation of the inevitable unyielding of her body, close, and with her eyes closed she tries and still fails to abandon all thought to the pleasure of his thrusts. She weeps as she tells him during the week they spend together while her mother drifts like an autumn leaf towards her end. "I don't understand. If I could understand, it would be all right . . . I don't understand the body. I don't understand why you want to make love to me. I don't understand, William. Can you help me?"

They are sitting at opposite ends of the table: beyond the window, the squalls of spring break the sea into foam monsters. Coriola has not wanted him to touch her.

"I don't know if I can help you. But I'd like to take your hand. You are really ugly when you cry," he says lightly, and kisses the tips of her fingers.

"I don't enjoy it."

"I know. I think she wrecked you," he adds, gripping her hand.

"But I never wanted her." Coriola is not sure as she shakes herself free of him and gets up from the chair if the tingling, the inability to sit still is anger, embarrassment or a raw nerve being touched.

"Exactly. What a bitch."

"I loved her. I cannot pretend I didn't. I cannot pretend she seduced me. I wanted to love her, it was just that my body did not respond. I didn't want her."

"Do you want me?"

"I do. My body doesn't. It's not that, I don't know what it is." Exasperated she turns to look out of the window: the clouds have broken to let swords of light onto the waves.

"It's something to do with not understanding what it is that we are doing when we"—she turns to face him—"when we make love. What does it mean?"

"You don't understand because she used you. And then you let yourself be used by everyone you met."

"Are you using me?"

"If I have, I don't want to anymore."

"Thank you," she says, sitting opposite him again. Sunlight is pouring in through the glass, showing up the lines on her face, making his eyes translucent.

"Can we love each other without making love?" she asks him.

"We'll try if you want."

"Do we have to make love?"

"We have to make"—he underlines the words—"and we can only make with what we have. And we have the body."

"It seems strange to say that we are 'making love.' How can a body make anything?"

"It's not the body. We are using the body. It's a means." He smiles.

She looks out of the window at the wind-swept sea and stares at the contradiction, thinking that behind it there is some further truth which she cannot see because her mind is deceived constantly by the flickering knowledge like the image on the eye that changes from vase to profile and back again. At seventy-five she knew that each image was illusion, and the truth lay somewhere, she thought, no longer seeking specificity, somewhere in the act, in the art, of looking. She saw that it was the same with lovemaking, the truth of it lay in the sudden brief unity of an act constructed from all the contradictory elements, and without the contradiction there could not be the encounter that resolves for an instant and dissolves in the next.

"It's also a game. Can't you play? You are afflicted with seriousness," he says seriously.

"Terrible, isn't it. What can I do?"

"Laugh."

"I do."

"Yes, but really."

"It doesn't do anything, it doesn't resolve anything. I still don't like it."

"Does not laughing make any difference?"

"No. It just seems more appropriate," Coriola says, suddenly laughing at the absurdity of it.

"Don't worry," William says lightly, sharing her sense of the ridiculous. She takes his hand.

"Your father said that," she says, rising from the chair.

"Did he make you laugh?" William asks as they walk out into the wind.

"Eventually . . ."

10

Onstage Coriola was serene: her body was the shell a real character penetrated gradually, filling every nook and cranny, poured into every interstice of bone and marrow, until the point of her toes, the top of her head, breasts, hips, crotch, lips, were inhabited. Her body was not flesh, though solid; matter displacing itself on the wooden boards, not flesh, leaden, lumpish flesh invaded by the flesh of another. It was an instrument, to speak words that could not be uttered except in the semblance of another, beshrew your eyes, they have o'erlooked me and divided me, words she had never spoken and would never speak in reality, she thinks at forty, looking at William on the other side of her mother's bed, absorbed in examining the brittle body; one half of me is yours, the other half yours—mine own, I would say; but if mine, then yours, and so all yours, she tells him silently, smiling into his serious eyes, suddenly raised from the bed where the mother has slid back into the sleep that prevents her from feeling too keenly the disease swelling her with an alien, chaotic life.

She was free onstage. Free to love, free to be, creating from the words a strong, tall, striding Portia. "Take thou," she said quietly, night after night for months, with the intensity of the quietly strong, "take thou thy pound of flesh, but in the cutting it, if thou dost shed one drop of Christian blood. . . ." And it did not matter that the script sometimes did not provide scope: Coriola, who had no imagination and could not fantasize—unlike Melissa, who at around this time met the father of her child and was discovering the world what would cut her off from the pleasure of reality—had an instinct for finding personality in the most unlikely words, and for suggesting the right words for characters Fanian, with whom she lived too many years, was trying to construct into plays from the poverty of his talent as a playwright, having refused to continue to use the talent he did have as a teacher in a large boys' school; having left the wife who could not love but had borne him two children.

"I am Fanian," he said, coming up to her at the beginning of rehearsals. Coriola saw a slender man with reddish hair and luminous brown eyes that were almost womanly in their largeness and the thickness of lash that framed them. His smile was broad and filled his face. She knew he had asked for her to play the main part, and though she had not particularly liked it, she could not afford to refuse it: she dreaded more intensely than ever the necessity to strip if she was not acting, like a drug to which she was addicted that brought temporary relief and permanent damage.

"Let's go," Fanian said a couple of hours later. There was no feature that reminded her of the doctor, she thought, feeling safe, though there was something in the way he held himself, she thinks at forty, she writes in winter while flakes of February snow accumulate like silence, that was like her father, rammed into death with Rita by his side, whom he had picked up a few miles before he flashed his light to overtake. He saw her on the side of the road and drew up from sudden curiosity.

"Get in," he said.

The girl did not thank him and climbed up without a smile next to him. He wondered whether he could stop a little later and thrust himself into her, thinking vaguely that she had been asking for it, standing so gauche on the grass verge, sullen thumb pointing.

"It's dangerous to hitchhike, a girl on your own."

Rita shrugged.

"I could be a rapist and a murderer," he added, glancing at her from the corner of his eye.

"You're not," Rita mumbled with the assurance of youth, turning her face away. She leaned her head against the window and, fleeing the domination of two mothers, the strangeness of seduction by one, immediately slept. He had barely time to feel a stir of protectiveness that made him slow down and throw his jacket over her sleeping form, before readjusting his mind to the familiar track—I will learn to love her in a new way as soon as I retire, as soon as I have time, he thought, seeing his wife's face—and flashed the light.

Coriola's mother was reduced to long silence, perhaps by the knowledge of the unknown adolescent next to the scarred remnants of her husband, seeing a lifetime of betrayals and young bodies lying obscenely by the side of every road, sprawled in readiness for his lust. The remains were never recognized as those of the daughter of the lady who lived so quietly with a woman friend behind net curtains in the corner house of a tree-lined street, each with her own room for appearances' sake, both with double beds no man ever visited, though Rita's mother sometimes, at conferences, had indulged the urge to feel a man inside her, a mustache, a beard on her breast. And yet those men, whose bodies she liked, the lovemaking, the speed of it, were all too strange, too incomprehensible. There was, she always thought, no possibility of companionship, and she left them stranded like beached whales, incapable of knowing what else she could get from them. They took what they could, her open legs, and felt little regret; somehow she wasn't right, they thought, returning to wives and girl friends, appreciating all the more whatever the quality was that made them want to return.

The riding instructress, protected from one kind of guilt by ignorance, consoled her lover with any resources at her disposal sharpened by another guilt.

"She'll show up," she told her, who wept with hair falling over red eyes and bloated features.

"She could have left me a note, told me why. Why did she go, my baby, why did she go?"—rocking inconsolably on kitchen chairs.

"It's our fault, she couldn't take us," she said, fidgeting with the curtains, looking up and down the silent Sunday street, imagining the gawky girl stomping between childhood and adulthood to the door.

"Of course that's not it, don't be ridiculous. She'll

write, she knows we worry, she'll write. She's an independent girl, that may indeed have been our fault. She knows how to handle things; she won't go under, she'll turn up in a week, maybe a little longer."

"Do you think so?" Tears, helpless tears poured down the mother's cheeks, helpless tears of hope.

And Rita would have undoubtedly returned, almost penniless and fifteen, Coriola writes, had she not got so far so quickly, so far the police could not put two and two together and identify the one charred obliterated face with the freckly, fringed creature of the photograph the mother carried to the station, immediately assuming from the horror in the wife's eyes at the news that the one, despite jeans and sweater and a duffle coat, had been a teenage hooker and the other a rebel: "Funny setup in that house. Maybe they're . . ." Putting index fingers together and winking, prurient among themselves while solemnly, seriously speaking to the distraught mother: "Yes, we've passed her photograph to all stations. We'll track her down, madam, don't worry."

Rita's mother cultivated through the years a cruelty towards her lover to punish her for her own sexuality, to punish herself for what she believed was the cause of her daughter's disappearance. And the riding instructress, knowing all too well, having secretly hired Desmond, the young red-haired detective whose innocent mien deceived all into revelation, sat in the park every sunny day looking at new generations of women, occasionally driven to approaching one, looked at increasingly askance by all, and returned to the house shrouded in net curtains, and to the woman she had betrayed, towards whom she was incapable of not feeling tenderness, begging to touch the wrinkled flesh of the soiled body; and when Rita's mother agreed, closed her eyes the better to conjure up images of litheness and taut skin, the faces that had stayed with her from the watchful hours by the playground where young mothers sat, where Jane came with the first, second and third child, glowing with the final fulfillment of motherhood, as content and placid as a tigress watching its cubs play in the shade. Jane still wore pink, tight-fitting skirts and high heels. She stained her hair blond, made love every day even after ten years of marriage and walked tall and arrogant among the other women whose husbands were in one way or another unsatisfactory: she did not consider herself lucky, believing what she received was merely her due, clouting husband and children over the ears if they did not live up to her expectations. But in the darkness and silence of night, in the quiet of late mornings, when her husband escaped from the nearby garage where he earned enough to keep them in meat a couple of days a week, she played teasing games of seduction and took pride in his swollen member, wanting him, wanting him, against a wall, on the kitchen table, on all fours on the frayed carpet, peacefully in the creaking double bed, thrusting and moaning. And they would rise, wrap themselves in worn gowns and celebrate their love with tea, in silence before he went back to the underbelly of a car and she ran to catch the bus and wait at the gates for her children scampering unkempt out of school. The school where Melissa taught, Melissa who, incapable of motherhood, had borne and left a copper-haired son in the hands of the father's sister, to be brought up among dark-haired siblings. At around the same time as Jane's eldest, she entered the other gate, her red curls straightened and severely pulled back, her face inevitably too pretty for the austerity of the hair, her wrists and hands too slender, too tender for the toughness in her eyes, a mask that gradually became real, causing confusion, a dislocation that left everyone who met her bewildered, uncertain of their ground: someone as pretty as she should be gentle, be teaching infants, be married. Not Head of Department in a school full of bullies who sometimes carried knives and scrawled obscenities on walls, blackboards and desks.

Ah, but it satisfied Melissa, the daily confrontation with those who could have crushed her neck with a hand and yet were subdued by the glint in her eye and the very fragility of her, who spent their afternoons in a cacophony of bars, talking among themselves endlessly of her, only rarely daring to speak their fantasy, seeing her unclothed and vulnerable . . . they would be gentle, not brutish as their friends required them to be; not knowing that Melissa liked the brutishness, not the gentleness that rose at the thought of her in the privacy of their teenage rooms plastered with posters of cars and motorbikes, where they unzipped and imagined her, slender legs apart, waiting for their—and too quickly, too inexpertly they came, while Melissa in the bedroom of the large comfortable flat taught herself the slow pleasure of mingled fantasies, to change from one scene in which one of them, Jane's eldest, saw her from his desk open and naked under the dress, superimposed immediately to the image of a group cornering her against the blackboard to rend blouse and skirt while the girls sat like statues, a mere background of still faces and empty eyes. She became increasingly bored with men's real touch, heavy breathing, blank eyes rolling in the sockets, the lack of pliability of real bodies that could not fly or dance or sway; that could not lie in tens on a vast bed under her as she stepped over their faces and lowered herself now on one, now on another long, large erection, all wanting her so much her mere approach would send seed spurting in a fountain; but one, faceless, she would fuck and fuck as they watched, until she was replete and sore on her solitary bed in the cool pale flat full of new objects she could not resist buying, accumulating trivia until the flat was stifled by it.

But that was later, long after Coriola's father's death, when Melissa had learned the lesson of solitude so well she was incapable of any but the most cursory encounters with men who invaded the cool rooms and disarranged the objects carefully placed on shelves and tables and bureaus, who brought dirt to the pale carpet, sweat to the bed, drops to the area around the toilet bowl, hairs to the basin; who made the flat small with loud voices and large shoulders; who refused at first to accept that she was not frightened at night on her own, that she was quite capable of mending a burst pipe and changing washers, but who, as soon as they could see it was true, retreated in panic at her independence, disappointed that though she was the best of lays, writhing shameless under and over them, their deepest desire, to be strong and capable, to protect, to bring to an end her fantasy life, could not be satisfied. The flat became ever lighter, like the inside of a shell, more orderly, the objects increased and displaced any man who saw her and wanted her, still pretty and fragile long after the morning of Coriola's mother's death when Coriola waits for grief by her mother's bed. She lifts the key from where it lies on top of a sealed envelope, the key that had lain under her mother's pillow until the nurses came to lay out the still-warm body. "For Coriola, instructions," the envelope says: the writing contains all the vibrations of weakness, reveals by its tremors the full extent of the disease that has reduced the body to such stillness. "Draw the curtains, promise," she said two days ago, before slipping into unconsciousness. Coriola goes to the window and pulls back the curtains, turns to look at her mother's dead body: yellow wax is molded into a wasted mask, but the lines of illness are smoothed, the features are definite, more definite in their stillness than they have ever been in a life that kept them shifting, from smile to laughter, from pain to plain. The blankets outline the bones. The hands lie on the coverlet: the fingers under the nails are white. What happens to the blood? The body dies; what happens to the blood? Does it become diluted into the fluids that will flow out of the body in the final humiliation? Will those fluids be red? What happens to the red blood? Her mother closed her eyes one last time, the heart stopped and blood turned to water. It was a good death, without agony, though with persistent murmurings, restless with tossings and reaching for disjointed words, messages without sequence—"Throw it away," "lock me," "short shrift," the insistent "draw the curtains, promise, draw the curtains."

It was a good death, Coriola thinks, returning to sit on the bed, weighing down the mattress with her pregnant body, tilting her mother's dead body, suddenly thinking she is not dead; she breathes, her chest rises and falls like mine. She is pretending. In a moment she will open her eyes and look at me, and the lines will re-form, the features lose their beauty, become hers. She watches, she waits for her mother not to be dead, for the hands to lift from the coverlet and cover her hand, resting uselessly by her side.

*A*t the end of the run as Portia, Coriola dressed in a man's suit and wandered the streets where at night she performed as a stripper. She sat in small cinemas with men on either side of her, in front and behind her, men who walked in sideways like crabs, afraid of recognition, darting eyes from side to side, leers of fearful excitement on their lips; men who came in twos, in threes, noisy and tipsy, laughing, pretending to themselves it was all a joke, dropping heavily in well-worn seats; men who strode looking neither to right nor left, severe, taut, rigid in their greed. She sat next to them, a man like them, through hours of storyless encounters of women with men, men with men, of women with women, women with animals, men with animals. At times in the hush of absorption, the occasional snort of excitement reaching a pitch, she felt laughter moving up from her belly like vomit, threatening to choke her, and she sneezed, coughed, rose and walked out, to look through peepholes at nude women standing as naked and empty-eyed as she did moving to a music in the club.

She watched, unflinching and without laughter, children like Melissa open to men who handled their prepubertal cunts; children like Melissa, like Desmond, touching, sucking the cocks of men, the cunts of women whose faces were invisible, hidden, cut off the screen; and shrugged off those who approached her at the exit thinking her a boy, their pupils hunting her from the corner of their eyes, their movements urgent, greedy, fearful. She returned to the club with icy relief and withdrew from promiscuity with the same abruptness with which at twenty-four she had chosen to live after a dream of a bar of chocolate proffered by her father. She had wanted to see if dressing as a man, acting like a man, she could see what man saw in the bare flesh of women opening and closing, hiding and revealing. What she saw was desecration, though it wasn't until she heard the word from Tom that she thought of using it, she thinks at forty-one, still beside her mother's body, returning her thought and gaze to the wasted flesh. It was a good death, she thinks again: somewhere at the back of her mind she laughs at the juxtaposition of words, and somewhere else she considers that she would have found nothing strange in the idea of death being good, only a year before. Love alone prevents her from recognizing the goodness of death: only the child with whom she is daily sharing life, who will soon take on life. And sitting by the body she is suddenly as rigid as her dead mother with terror at the hourly possibility for desecration her child will have to endure, and the final desecration that she is responsible for handing down to it by giving it life, flesh turned to cold wax, blood to water. She doesn't know, as tears stream down her cheeks and splash, large and wet, on her domed belly, whether she is crying for her mother or for her unborn child. Or is she, in the end, she wonders, lifting the stiff hand to kiss, leaning over to smooth the already smoothed skin on the face, removing soft locks of incongruous, rich brown hair from her mother's forehead, weeping for herself? For her own absence from a world she has made to fit her own needs, just as she makes her own image in the mirror, a world only at moments revealed as being other, not contained by her, but in which she is contained like a more or less useful object in a box of odds and ends?

At forty Coriola rises from the deck chair at the sound of the doorbell. Summer has stroked color into her cheeks and penetrated the cotton dress to warm her flesh. She strides towards the enclosed terrace house among towering buildings where her mother has lived since the death of her husband, through the small garden where weeds stand taller than the dozen rosebushes her mother planted before Coriola returned home and their life was brought to a curious standstill. Nothing happened: the mother walked to town every week to collect her pension; Coriola sold clothes in a little boutique. Occasionally someone would frown: where had they seen her face? But it was merely that everyone, crisscrossing the streets, became familiar with habitual faces, and it was seeing it in a different context, behind a counter rather than striding long-limbed. Morning and evening Coriola went to and from her job, smiling a smile empty but for the fragment, the small fragment, where Tom lodged in her heart—Tom, whom she had met again on the train during the long journey from one end of the country to the other, who had told her to go home to the seamless days. Mother and daughter waited for something, a break in the sequence of day succeeding day without a hitch, too empty and meaningless for the energy required to encourage life. But life insisted, sprawling itself wildly wherever there was an inch of earth to permit its survival, in between the cracks in the paving stones, in the moist corners of the walls of the house. Coriola today has lain in the chaos rejoicing, unwilling to disturb the weeds, such proof of persistence, such proof of the necessity and validity of hope, that pushes grass and bracken, moss and creeper from the earth towards the sun, that opens roses, that unfolds fern and leaf to play with the wind for a season, that spills itself into the abundance of briar and flower, insect and beast. That has compelled Coriola to yield.

"You are so hard. There is no tenderness," William has said a few hours before. "I don't understand your fierceness," he adds, pacing the room.

The windows are open to catch the evening breeze, moonlight fades on the carpet, ousted by the lamps on either side of the sofa where Coriola perches, following William with her eyes.

"Nor I you," she says.

"Why are you so hard?"

"I don't know. I'm not."

"You don't give. I mean of yourself. You are rigid even when we make love."

William pauses as Coriola rises and walks to the window. She looks out at the moon.

"Don't slide your eyes away," he adds.

"No," Coriola agrees, turning, looking at him straight in the eye, defiant, desperate. "I don't like it. I've told you enough times." She turns her back to him before asking, "Shall we break off?"

William is exasperated. "No, no, no. Why do you always take the easy way out?"

"Is it?"

"Of course it is. I want to break through, to you. God only knows why, but I love you."

A blush races up from her crotch to her face at the words. Slowly she turns to face him. They stand across the room from each other, equally tall, equally dark, in light summer clothes of clashing patterns, he in white trousers and red shirt, she in a yellow dress with flower patterns.

"You love me?"

"Looking at you makes me feel uncomfortable," she adds after a second; her voice shakes.

"Only because you're not used to it. You've avoided looking at anyone."

William comes no nearer, but fixes her with the same relentless eyes as his father.

"There is nothing except moments outside each other." Coriola turns back to face the moon.

"That's not true."

"I can't believe you."

"Can't you trust me?"

"No."

"What are you protecting?"

Coriola is silent. She can feel his eyes on her, willing her to turn.

"Nothing. There is nothing to protect," she says softly.

"Are you protecting the fact that there is nothing to protect?"

Coriola throws back her head and laughs, but the laughter finishes in a hard rasping sound, the dry sob of tears that have failed.

"Can't you let go?"

Impatient, restless, Coriola paces the room: the sofa is now a bulwark between them. William watches her move, cold as ice in his love.

"I dare you."

Suddenly Coriola feels a weariness identical to the weariness she felt at twenty-four looking at her skeletal shadow on the pavement. The hands she has held clutched in the pockets of her dress fall by her side; her shoulders drop, her thighs push for support against the back of the sofa, and she looks at William.

"Could you go now? Leave? Please?" Coriola barely breathes the words.

William shakes his head. "No. I love you."

For a second time, at the second avowal, a blush moves across her body like a ray of sun emerging from behind clouds.

"I'm afraid," she tells him, her voice shaking again.

"So am I," William answers.

At seventy-five Coriola could still feel William's control over his body, which would have moved forward, would have taken her into his arms if he had not known, sensed, that it was Coriola who had to make her act of hope, of faith; who had to walk around the sofa and allow herself to be taken. At forty Coriola cannot analyze, petrified of the certainty of love he is offering her, standing taller than she, larger than she, infinitely more sure than she could ever be. Like an animal paralyzed by headlights, she faces him across the room.

"Help me, William," she whispers.

"I am. I will."

His voice is gentler than she has ever heard it, his eyes bore into her, and Coriola, like a child taking its first steps, drawn like a magnet by the solidity of him, moves one step, two steps, rounds the sofa and is finally against him, her face buried in his chest. His comforting hands are on her hair, stroking her back. She can feel him erect against her, knows herself dilated and straining for him. Clumsily they part, but only to switch off the two lamps, to remove underwear, to unzip urgently. They slide awkwardly onto the sofa, but it is too narrow, and they slide farther down onto the carpet, where Coriola can see the ironic full moon before abandoning thought for the unique, intense pleasure of her lover's touch, before closing her eyes and letting herself finally go with the image of her lover's father's eyes, looking at her straight, shaking her hand for the last time: "Don't ask too many questions. Relax. It's all right."

"It's all right," she murmurs to William. He opens his eyes as she shuts hers and allows herself to come for the first time, and the slow, exquisite orgasm radiates out almost painfully to every part of her body, as if her flesh were indeed melting.

A few hours later her heart hammers, a blush covers the color the sun has given her, her hands sweat as she opens the door. She looks at him with a shyness she has never before felt and instantly smiles, laughs to recognize the same shyness in his eyes, the same blush on his face, the identical hammering of his heart against her heart, the erection insistent, her own crotch immediately wet with desire.

12

I'll think better on a train, she told herself at thirty-seven. He won't be able to reach me.

I'll just stay on the train forever, she said, packing toothbrush, some dresses, a couple of skirts, three pairs of shoes, boots, the heavy coat, going out to buy comfortable cotton pants and bras, leaving behind flimsy underwear, lacy camisoles.

I'll go back and forward, cross-country. I'll go through every station, catch every local and live on trains. Keep moving. Mustn't stay still.

She spoke to herself, told no one—though who was there to tell, she asks herself at forty: Fanian had swallowed the possibility of acquaintances, friendships, any contact greater than the chilly grey good morning and good evening of strangers who need to use each other.

She boarded trains, sat in corner seats by the window, idle hands in her lap, staring at changing landscapes through curtains of rain, veils of mist, occasional bright days when the winter sun on the glass blinded her and she was compelled to shut her eyes and observe the wild gnats created by light on closed lids; lulled by the rocking of the train, quieted by the indifference of passengers who came, sat briefly opposite her, got off at the next station, men and women who, she was amazed to realize, lived lives that bore no relation to her own: talking, the women, of fêtes and children, the making of jams, chutneys, tarts, this recipe, that meal, their plans for Christmas, the presents they had bought; the men sat silent, staring ahead, once or twice glancing in her direction with curiosity, and if they came on board in pairs, never chattered like the women but made monosyllabic statements she had no way of understanding, not being familiar with or interested in farming, crops, the details of a world that had revolved, all her life, parallel to her own. She felt the same shock she had felt losing weight in her grandmother's house, to see outside herself lives that were not her own, and the terror of seeing herself through binoculars, tiny, clear and distant in a world swarming with people who might or might not experience what she had experienced took over from the relief at the anonymity of constant movement, stations, waiting rooms, timetables she pored over to plot the slowest, the longest route with the greatest number of stops, combing the country like a police patrol looking for clues at the site of a murder; combing the country for clues. But clues to what?

She had stayed with Fanian too long; that she could have stayed with him at all was as strange as the purposeless existence, in the depth of the sea, of darting monstrous creatures that never see light and are never seen. He told Coriola, when it was too late for her to escape, that he had seen her, long before Portia, performing in the pub and had been determined to "own" her: he spoke those exact words, laughing, his eyes luminous brown, incapable of entering her, losing strength as soon as he saw her open legs on the bed, unless he had a camera. With a camera he took endless pictures of her body, shaved of womanhood, wearing a gamut of clothing at various stages of undress, of various periods, clothes taken from greenrooms or hired. He masked the face with handkerchiefs, a pillow; the hair he demanded she grow, and laughed, erect, in anticipation of showing the obscene shots to others, watching their reaction and satisfying himself with the memory of their expression coupled with stills to which he added, he told her, laughing, the face of any young child who had caught his eye and the eye of the camera he took with him everywhere, tucked in the pocket of his jacket. They never made love, but in her obsession the striptease acquired a greater intensity, as if she were making love to him by stripping for him, who sometimes allowed her to touch him, to pour the last of her draining tenderness on the member that only rarely rose and spilled seed; and then only outside her, separate from her, while Fanian grinned ironically at her, lying back on the bed: in the train she opened and shut her eyes against the remembered look, shook her head, stared out of the window.

Then she left him as abruptly as she has done everything except move to William's arms, she thinks at forty, the morning she realizes she is pregnant and the first wind of autumn, contained, hidden in the late August day, moves the leaves to a more brittle rustle. Coriola would like to dance through her fear, to dance her fear away, but she walks calmly to her dying mother and her lover.

"I am pregnant," she tells him. His face is still for a fraction, then splinters into joy.

"It must have been that night," she says to him, safe in his arms, lifted by him, dancing with him, all fear gone which will return, which she will set herself to conquer, slowly, slowly, step by step, not seeking his help, not needing any more help than to know he is there and would take her hand. All the help she needs is to know she is present to him. And now she is as strong as a lion to conquer her fear, she thinks. She has not spoken of Fanian to him, merely telling him the bare facts. "We lived together, if you can call his goings and rare comings living together, for four, almost five years. I lusted for him." She is still surprised at the lust, never experienced before, never experienced since. It is certainly not lust she feels for William, she writes, though she treasures his body, though she treasures the touch that has, mysteriously, for the first time, opened her. Though she treasures the particular calm of him, the safety of him, the fact that she can be as sure of him, of the value of him, as of a hoard of jewels, and therefore that she can finally let go, spend of herself like the most profligate of millionaires, knowing there is always more. There is, and will be, him. It is a strange thought, that they can kiss lightly and pass by without hunger and anxiety because of the certainty that came unbidden, unsought in the summertime, months after she met him on the day she accompanied her mother to the hospice, shook hands with the young doctor, not knowing the man who cared for the dying was the son of the man who saved her from death, though his surname had made her heart miss a beat. She was struck by his silence and his strong hands as he flanked her mother on the way to the room overlooking the grounds that would be her home for a year. He walked Coriola back to the car, and she asked him, looking at the grey eyes on the unlined face, if he was the son of the father she had known.

She conquered death at twenty-four through the coldness of faith of the doctor. She conquered her obsession with Fanian through a coldness of hope, opening her eyes after the glare of the sun had forced them shut to see, sitting opposite her in the musty carriage, a tall gaunt Benedictine who recognized her before she recognized him.

"Coriola," he said, his smile like the smile of a child, though the lines on his face told stories he would never disclose.

"Tom." For a time she could only repeat his name, as if he were a vision. Tears she had not wept throughout the month she had been living in trains from one station to the next slid down her cheeks like a summer storm against glass. He came and sat next to her—the other passengers, an embarrassed couple, stared before rising and leaving the compartment, and Tom pulled down the blinds, held her hand while she wept, gave her the handkerchief.

"Stay with us," he told her. "Let's get off at our station, come to us," he said.

She was led to the monastery, given a small bare

room, white, where she could weep, given the freedom of icy woods where she tramped in borrowed boots, from where she could hear, when the wind was in the right direction, men's voices raised in plaintive chant: she stood still at the sound, aware of voices dispersing in the world, losing their power, growing weaker and weaker, raised uselessly to an indifferent sky. Who was to blame? Was there blame to be attached? At what point could Fanian have been said to have chosen to be what he was? Was it not as accidental as the accumulation of accidents that had fashioned her? Had she not become who she was by the effect on her of her mother's voice when she had thrown a beaker, by the tone of voice when she had said, Don't do, Don't say, by Desmond being slapped across the room and a father who could never explain why he had done it, by a riding instructress who had taken her to her bed as a result of a chain of arbitrary circumstances, by her own inexplicable passion for starvation? At what point were cause and effect no longer relevant? Was her starvation linked to the riding instructress, her obsession with Fanian linked to the riding instructress? If she had not been the kind of baby who threw beakers across rooms, perhaps none of it would have happened? And if Fanian had not been the kind of child— What kind? Coriola tried to remember things Fanian said that would explain what he was, looked at the possible circumstances that could have fashioned the man she had known, and no element seemed to fit. What series of accidents made him the man who could only, only . . .

"Abuse?" suggested Tom, with whom she sat, who walked with her at times through the cold afternoons.

School? A lonely childhood? Perhaps he would not have realized the intensity of his desire for prepubescent girls if he had not looked out of the window at the playground just at the moment when, lit up as if by a spotlight, Melissa's legs were in the air, the dress and vest back over her head, the tummy bare and the white cotton panties ridiculously alluring. And the shock would not have driven him into marriage with a woman who could not love, and if he had not married her, if he had not changed schools, perhaps he would not have felt it necessary to carefully construct an alternative person who rejoiced in the vulnerability of emotion because he could not possess the vulnerable body of a child.

Coriola at forty-one balks at the disproportion of circumstances and consequence. It explains nothing, she thinks. The fixed gaze can see beyond all reflections, farther and deeper into the darkness to a shifting blankness, a mass of unknowing that gives when pressed like cotton wool, only to refashion itself just beyond reach, constantly elusive, constantly deluding one into a search for explanation: did she not perhaps make Fanian into the man he was with her, pushing him into further and further violations, egged him into humiliating her by her acceptance of the first abuse, by her passivity when the others followed, accumulated, became as inescapable as an addiction? Does not a love that submits totally, that turns the other cheek, torture the recipient into more elaborate tests? Is not love too dangerous, Coriola asked Tom, who listened to the broken accounts of a life, who gave her, by his existence, something that dared not be hope.

"Those who love put themselves in danger. If you are

given, the person to whom you are given may do you harm."

"But is that love? Can that be love?"

"It is one form, an extreme form. Some are apt to love so. You are apt to love so."

At seventy-five she moved weakly in the bed, weakened further by pity and terror, knowing what Coriola at thirty-seven could not, what Coriola at forty-one cannot yet glimpse at, that the lust she felt at thirty-two was simply a different manifestation of the passion for starvation, the intensity of hatred for the body, the incomprehension at life driving her to taunt and tease herself closer and closer to death: at twenty she had starved her body, at thirty-two she had used the body she had starved at twenty to starve her soul, to deny life in a new way. Her obsession with Fanian was not love, but a confirmation, in his attitude to her body, of her own attitude to it. Violation and starvation were two sides of the same coin, Coriola knew at seventy-five, having learned the habit of happiness, having learned from William the inescapability of being body, having fought slowly to make from what was inescapable something radiant, as one might direct light into the darkest corner by the use of mirrors; and from it having learned beyond inescapability the necessity to be body; having had it confirmed by Tom at fifty-eight, after the dam burst into tears, in the exhausted companionship of a grief shared, who told her that her mother had baptized her over the bath when as a baby she thrust her fingers into an electric socket.

A toddler, crawling in the first exuberance of discovery, muttering baby talk to herself, she approached the whiter projection on the pale wall behind the table from which a thread seemed to hang, was momentarily distracted by a stubborn piece of fluff that had not been sucked up by the noisy machine her mother was using, and settled down to play, changing from the all fours of movement to the seated position, her back straight, proud of the recently acquired balance, proud that the head was not too heavy, dragging her forward. She stretched small fingers and pulled the plug, bent forward to look more carefully, always with fingers so much more adept at exploration than the puzzled eyes, and pushed them into the socket just as her mother switched off the machine and turned to check on her. She hardly cried when the shock went through her, but her mother in terror beyond comprehension saw the little body twist in epilepsy and lie still under the table.

"Coriola, Coriola," she shouted, her voice inhuman with fear. Time slowed down, stood still, to allow the terror to cut through to the marrow of her bone, slowed down to give her all the time in the world to think, She's dead, my baby whom I love because I have not really wanted her; I must baptize her, my baby. I—God, don't let her be dead. And slowly, in the expansion that transforms seconds into minutes, minutes into hours, the mother scooped up the white body, slapped it violently—Breathe, damn you, breathe, will you. Don't die, I cannot live with the guilt of your death. I must baptize her; and immediately she was upstairs, in the bath, pouring water over the baby's face: I baptize you in the name of the father, who must have mercy on my sin, and of the Son, who died that you may not, and of the Holy Spirit, who must be the breath of your little life that I may not live in guilt. And she kissed the baby's mouth and felt light, slight, miraculous, the trace—the illusion?—of moist breath.

Now time took on speed: quick, quick, to the hospital. Neighbors, friends, anyone, save me from her little death. The large blanket was over her, Coriola was in a cocoon of blanket, and her mother, tripping over the trailing material, was out, talking to the first person she met, unknown, never seen again. The woman put a large hand on her shoulder.

"Calm yourself. You must."

The voice was low, slow. She lay the baby on the ground, on the pavement, cushioned in the blanket, knelt, a giant, over her and pressed against a chest the width of her four fingers, put large lips on tiny lips, covering chin and nose, pushing breath into Coriola, pressing the heart to beat because death is a monster to be avoided, because death will cause too much guilt. And the color returned to the lips warmed by the stranger's lips, to the cheeks rubbed, slapped.

"She'll be okay now. We'll ring the hospital. You're in shock. Come, we'll make some tea. Is there some brandy, whiskey, anything? For the baby too?"

And the woman held the mother who clutched the baby, incapable yet of the full realization that only love could have induced the agony of the last few moments that were hours in her life, streaking her young face with the first line, her dark hair with the first white one, making her shake, shake for minutes that gradually returned to accurate sixty seconds, each second shorter than a breath, than the precious breath of life.

* * *

Coriola at forty-one lifts her face to the window out of which her mother gazed. She looks at the trees, at the leaves vibrating in the breeze: newly green leaves of a new, inescapable spring. As inescapable as any winter. She wipes her cheeks with the sleeve of her mother's nightdress, anointing her dead flesh with tears, and lays the hand back on the white coverlet before walking heavily to the window and opening it. The breeze moves through her to the bed and ruffles her mother's hair.

13

"*I*f there are men, people like you,
maybe it's worth it," Coriola found herself saying to Tom
at thirty-seven.

"If there are women, people like you, it's definitely
worth it," he answered, chewing a first blade of grass, on
a bench in the spring sun.

"I could fall in love with you," she said.

"I have." He smiled.

The simplicity of it stayed with her as she organized
a new life from the safety of her white room to the safety
of the narrow room, determined not to put into thought
the question that at forty, still in winter, she puts into
writing, What does it mean to say I could fall in love with
you? Is it any more than to say I need the comfort of the
knowledge of your existence in a world that is too dark
and empty and comfortless?

"Don't be alone. Go to your mother; I've told her you

are here. She was worried, not having heard from you for so long." She thought perhaps she and her mother could . . . what? At forty-one, sitting on the bed the afternoon of her mother's burial in the small Catholic cemetery, surrounded by the tipped contents of the drawers, she wonders what exactly she had thought she and her mother could have given each other, separated by a silence that had the depth of a sea and the width of a sky.

She has emptied the moth-scented wardrobe and added to the pile the few dresses, the skirts, the shoes. Stephen and Peter have left, rushing in grief and relief back to the bustle of their lives, but Coriola, her belly large with William's seed, looks at the objects chosen so carefully to remain and reveal. Her brothers have not been interested, though momentarily stunned by the discovery of their mother's Catholicism, hidden like the rosary at the back of the bottom drawer, behind a black missal, like objects of a depraved perversion.

"All those months at the hospice, she left these things. Just these things," she tells William. "The locked door. It's all so deliberate. There are letters . . ." She shows him two parcels, one of typed envelopes tied securely with string, the other a bulky white envelope, new, unlabeled. He picks up one of the dresses.

"Try it on," he asks her.

"I'm too big."

"Come on, try it. It looks your size."

"She's the last person I would have imagined to have become a Catholic."

But when William opens the thick white envelope, while Coriola slips into her mother's dress, silk and satin threads of various blues, that slides like a caress over her tall frame and domed belly, he finds a baptismal certificate, a confirmation certificate, photographs of a tall father, a fragile mother, children, a boy and a girl holding hands, a baby; another attractive woman with hair that would be red and looks a lighter shade of dark in the black-and-white photos; a boy growing from childhood to early manhood, staring at the camera from large luminous eyes, impenetrable eyes.

"She became a Catholic before she married." He points to the documents.

"You look spectacular in that dress," he says, looking at her again, the document still in his hand, the photographs still hidden in the envelope. Panic blocks Coriola's throat, sudden, uncontrollable, incomprehensible.

"There is no mirror," she says, her voice high.

"Good, you'll just have to take my word for it." William takes her hand that trembles. Her heartbeat shimmers on the dress.

"Look, see the documents, she was nineteen." His hand is firm, reassuring. Coriola breathes deeply, quiet, quiet against the panic of no immediate reflection to confirm or deny what he says. She sits on the bed and looks at the certificates.

"Why did she never say?"

"Perhaps it was never important until the end."

But the wooden beads worn small and smooth and the black missal frayed by fingering speak otherwise.

Tom confirmed, eighteen years later, that he had sat near the fishpond in the shade of the sycamore at eighteen, the summer Coriola and Stephen spent with their grandmother, and talked to her mother about his vocation while Coriola's younger brother enjoyed his last summer as a child, chasing a friend with a gun, bang bang you're dead: the following year Peter began to feel awkward, too tall to play, too young to do anything except sit around waiting for whatever transformation was necessary to end the discomfort of a sliding voice, the down on the cheek more obtrusive, a shadow on the chin and upper lip, an embarrassing bulge that forced him to change his attitude to clothes, making him most often self-conscious and occasionally proud. The following year Coriola's life plunged into a nightmare of mirrors. But this summer Tom, soothed from the ache of his desire for Kate, sat with Coriola's mother and imagined himself in love with her.

"See," she said, "how time has concertinaed for us. You are as young as my daughter, and yet I feel we are of the same age." She told him of her faith but kept her belief hidden from everyone else.

"I've thought about it for years. I asked her at eighteen, and she shrugged and smiled. I wrote to her a few times, tried to convince her when you came to us that winter, but she made me promise I would not tell you."

There was no way to explain it. She had talked enthusiastically of the good the world would receive from the sacrifice of his life, and Tom was not sure at fifty-eight how much his decision at eighteen was made to please her, how far he had embarked on it as a sacrifice to her.

"But it must have been right in many ways or I would not have stayed. I don't regret it," he later told Coriola, still reeling from William's death in a flood at a far mountain village where he had gone walking with Tom.

Tom sat by her in her desolation, silent at first and gradually talking, to prise from her tears that would heal but for days and weeks refused to come, blocked by a much better dam than the one that burst and dragged William, tumbled William against rocks, buried William under inches of mud, maybe still alive, William's nose, William's mouth filling with earth, unable to breathe— Coriola could not breathe at the thought, sharing in the torture she invented for him, who had died within seconds of the impact of water, hitting his head against the first rock, and felt nothing except surprise; but Coriola suffered moments of increasingly shallow breath, short gasps, raspings with open mouth in search of air, experienced even the raw taste of mud, grit at the back of the throat blocking the movement of the tongue . . .

Months later she wept against Tom, against the rough serge of a black habit that smelled of long use without indulgence, and was rocked in his arms as she had been rocked in her father's, her mother's arms when she emerged from her nightmare at twenty-four. Her tears were a sea of mourning for all loss by all people in all the world, from the beginning to the end of time, for her own loss of her grandmother at twenty-two, her father at thirty; for her mother, for whom she cannot weep again at forty-one, too bewildered by her mother's life, as she looks at the documents, the deliberate selection of objects, as she unties the tight knots on the larger of the two parcels and unfolds letters, shocked as she spreads out photographs of Fanian, as she unfolds letters from Fanian. Her hands are icy, and the baby inside her belly leaps in protest at the tightening of the muscles, at the pace of her heart, and she remembers the willfully forgotten words whispered by her mother, dying: "Don't, the key. Draw the curtains, promise." She stares at the signature on letter after letter, but without reading them, fearful to go beyond the "Darling," and "Dear," and "Sweetheart" that head each one, from the first childish scrawl, more than thirty of them; she stares at the photographs, image after image of the same child, boy, man who had been brother and lover, her own lover and uncle. Or was he her . . .

"What is it?" William asks, looking at her pale lips. "Are you all right?"

No, it cannot be, her tallness, her features, her coloring, all came from her father, the father who gave her chocolate in a dream and dragged her back into life.

"Coriola, are you all right?"

"Yes, it's nothing. It's these letters." He must not know. Secret. Buried, burned, past; be oblivion.

"Are these your mother's parents? Her brothers?" His movements are slow in Coriola's sight as he picks up photographs. "Nice-looking boy. Your uncle?" His voice is remote, muffled. She wills her own voice not to shake, her body not to slide, her mind not to slip.

"Yes. I never actually met either of them. Or her parents." The lie. The first. The lie. Why had her mother chosen so deliberately to tell her, why had she not wanted to die without letting her know they—she and her brother— they had—they—she and her mother had shared the same man, uncle, brother? Her mother who had so carefully thrown out things, making bonfires in the overgrown garden, standing by them, bent and fragile, blowing to warm her hands, accepting the death to come, stripping herself of all, not wanting Coriola to help, refusing her offer at least to carry objects, papers, things to the brightly burning pyre. "No, I'll do it myself," coughing down the steps, locking the door on the secret. But not locking the secret into the past, not burning the secret, not making the past into nonexistence. Deliberately, carefully choosing to tell her after her death, leaving key, notebook and envelope on the bedside table, waiting to be wax before inflicting on her daughter the burden of her, the burden. Sin. Sin. The word whispers itself as she smiles to hide herself from her lover, walking with him to the front door of her mother's house to let him return to the hospice to care for others who still have to die, whispers itself as she retraces heavy steps. Sin. Her own, she did not throw the key away, willfully forgot her mother's words. Sin. She knows nothing except the word, dredged from she knows not where by the new knowledge of her mother's Catholicism, the surprise as she read the instructions: the plot already bought, many years before, before Coriola returned home at thirty-seven, the coffin chosen and paid for; don't, the instructions seemed to say, don't trouble yourselves to choose pine or mahogany, beech or birch, brass or steel, to show your love. The priest chosen, a little mean man who scuttled through the service, paid for so many masses for the repose of her soul. And he took the money and will not pray, Coriola thinks. He, too, deliberately chosen by a mother so steeped in guilt she thought there was no hope. Why pray at all then? Why not let her body be thrown away with no recognition, be furnace fodder?

Coriola sits in her mother's dress, shivering in the chilly room. Did her mother know that throughout the

years she was with Fanian, while Peter traveled and returned from distant parts, while Stephen's wife, who had
borne Ann before Coriola's father smashed into death,
bore a son who died within weeks, in his cot early one
morning, minutes after his mother had seen him sleeping
the deep sleep of babyhood, while Melissa pursued her
road to solitude and Jane hers to the awe-full simplicity
of physical love transformed into companionship, while
Desmond gave seed to his high-heeled wife from which
she fashioned children, temporarily content in flat shoes
and support bras, quickly, defiantly perching on stillettos
and letting the world rejoice in the glory of her breasts,
even larger with milk; while Fanian's wife enjoyed the
company of two sons and the absence of men; while unknown children became men and women, men and women
aged, the aged died and some, a few, were cared for by
William, a young medical student who had no perception
of the depth of comfort he was bringing by the evident
sympathy in his eyes, who watched his father succumb
to an illness that reduced him to a leaf permanently shaken
by a wind that touched nothing else; did Coriola's mother,
who retreated farther and farther into a silence no one
knew was filled with the rattle of beads and the mutterings
of prayers, know that throughout those years, Coriola
returned to the club for Fanian, who could only become
erect if he was among the audience watching other men
watching her strip?

Coriola sits in her mother's room: never will she tell
William, so dark and safe, that throughout the time she
and Fanian—she stumbles over the word, over the memory, unwilling to look again at years compared to which

the nightmare of starvation was merely a dream, pulling the bedspread, scattering the photos to the floor, wrapping herself against the cold knowledge, certain suddenly as she lies back, holding her bellyful of life, that whatever her mother's motive for finally revealing the truth, Fanian had played with mother and daughter, that his relationship had been, as well as perverse, a refinement of cruelty towards his sister, who had tried, who had eventually succeeded in rejecting the expression of her love for him.

"Yes, it was sin." Tom confirmed, as the words "incest," "evil" spilled from her with her tears eighteen years later. William died because of her, because of a mother's sin visited upon the daughter to the third, to the fourth generation. "No, no," Tom told her, Tom who left the monastic life at sixty to share with Coriola the aging of their bodies, the slowing of their minds, the perennial quickening of the heart. They lay and touched each other with a pleasure closest to the pleasure the twelve-year-olds had experienced stripping for each other in the greenhouse; they were in each other's company in a way closest to the way Coriola had been with Melissa at ten.

"Why, then, why did he die? It was my sin; my sin killed him. Why did she tell me, Tom? Tom, why not bury the past? Why did I forget, did I forget, her words, 'promise,' 'the key'?"

"Hush, hush, I don't know. Some things we can never know. But perhaps it was best to know, that you should know."

Coriola sits in her mother's room, her hands still, helpless with regret, the unalterability of the past present to her in the image of Fanian still clear, vivid as color is vivid in a dream, his head slightly tilted to the left, one leg forward, the careful trousers carefully pressed, the tie bright, belying the severity of the suit, forever stretching his hand to her and leading her through years that for all eternity are carved into time like graffiti on a marble pietà: her mother, sister and lover of her daughter's lover, had not blinked an eyelid, pretending not to know Fanian when they visited at Christmas, sliding beads through her fingers, secretly bowing her head in church at the tinkle of a bell: This is my body given. Her body given. And not to blink an eyelid, not to come and say to her daughter— ah, but what could she say? She had been lover of her mother's lover, brother. What could her mother say, do? At seventy-five Coriola was conscious that one component, one absurd, one ridiculously obscene element of her reaction to the revelations at forty-one, was jealousy; she could hardly lift a hand, helpless in the face of the mystery, the existence of creatures, human, doomed to weaving a cross-hatch of emotions that was beyond complexity in its design and revert to fathomless simplicities in the end, in the puny gesture of lifting heart and mind, hardly lifted, in atonement, and knew her mother's gesture had spread like waves from a stone thrown, reaching and spreading through Coriola's life from before her birth to beyond her death.

14

At forty-one, in the quiet moments before day gives way to night, Coriola lies still under the bedspread, still incapable of warmth, staring into the lengthening shadows patterning the walls and the floor of her mother's room. She thinks she will never move again, but horror gives way, ebbs like a wave, leaving as debris the silence of knowledge, and inexorable life stirs: the baby in her womb kicks, claims her, demands her days, years, claims her life as its own, to be given right and wrong, daily contradictions and absurdities, winters and summers, cold and heat. Love. Coriola stretches stiffened limbs that have lain rigid in the cold room, and without understanding she picks from the floor each photo, each letter, and methodically, slowly, she tears through the luminous eyes, the characterless script, pushing revulsion aside, tearing from herself with each piece a fraction of the regret that would otherwise clothe her like a matte paint that absorbs all light.

And when all the evidence of a love that was mirror and image of her own—whether or not it took the same form in its expression, she inserts months later, waiting for her daughter to wake for the next feed, about to grace the room and the world with cries of hunger and sighs of satisfaction, about to renew for her mother the pleasure of toothless gums gnawing at the breasts, lips sucking— when all the evidence of the distortions of love is a mound of fragments on the bedspread, she gathers them, walks down the stairs and into the sodden garden where last year's growth is now a brown pulp that in a few weeks, miraculously, as Coriola gives birth, will also give birth to a new rainbow of greens. In the empty garden, slowly, ritually, she makes an altar of bricks on which to lay all that has refused to say yes to life, piles on it the destroyed letters and photos and sets a match to them. She stands by the bonfire, warmed by the fast-curling paper, features, letters reduced to ash, drained and empty, but knowing her body is full and William waits to fill her heart.

And when all that remains of her and her mother's past is a small litter of ash, she strides back into the house, removes the mirror from her own room and takes it to her mother's room. In front of it she strips off her mother's dress to observe the beauty of her body, the breasts large in anticipation of birth, their skin and the skin of her belly transparent, showing the violet veins of blood; the legs strong to carry the burden, the child who, as Coriola at seventy-five quieted her soul towards the death of her body, held her hand or laid it on her own belly to make her mother touch new life leaping in the womb. The cohorts of the dead encouraged Coriola, turning and beckoning, sudden smiles in the mist of dreams where she flailed and fought: her small grandmother talking of flowers without words; her grandfather in the full grandeur of height restored; her father still shadowy, silent, burdened with eyes that did not look and yet could see; Peter, a child carrying a kite, whose bones had wasted away ten years before in a distant country; Melissa, who at ninety, free of her fantasy world, sat next to Tom in an old-people's home, cared for by brisk nuns speaking soft brogue, not knowing her story was written but relishing the visitors he received with immaculate courtesy: a scowling teenager whose rare smile flooded the ward with sunlight, who came with a handsome middle-aged woman, "My wife's daughter," Tom told Melissa proudly, the pale eyes momentarily a deeper green; Stephen who died two years after Coriola; Stephen's daughter, whom William had passionately loved before dying, from whom he had fled to the mountains in order to resume fidelity to the wife of his youth: Ann, who smiled at Coriola beyond time, gentle like her mother, who had rung William the evening before the flood to say she carried his child, had come to the funeral pale and utterly composed, had borne a son, never married, and also came to sit by Tom and Melissa, bringing flowers and chocolates for which both had insatiable, childish greed, came sometimes accompanied by a young man whose eyelids drooped at the corner. Sometimes the young man came on his own; and on a couple of occasions, he bumped into the mother and daughter he did not know were his sister and niece, from whom he and his mother had drifted apart though he remembered clearly, fifteen years before, visiting his dying aunt and the blush that would race up his spine at the sight of Coriola's pregnant daughter, his unknown sister, whom he somehow could not prevent himself from seeing naked, her round belly on which the heavy breasts rested hiding the pudenda. Who knows that the story did not continue with William's son meeting his twenty-year-old niece five years after Tom's and Melissa's deaths. Or perhaps he traveled to the distant country where Peter had fathered a daughter, unbeknown to him who had spent only one night with the mother. And Coriola's granddaughter met Fanian's grandson: thanks to the care of a grandmother who, long after the desertion of her husband, discovered a love that had no need to be expressed through sordid contact of bodies and slid into place in a world that thrives and perpetuates itself by tension and contradiction, he, unlike his grandfather, could build with Irene an instant that shone like a yellow fragment of stained glass against the sun, and call to Coriola, beckoning.

At seventy-five Coriola looked beyond life, where time is no more, where neither is there weeping. She looked to William, who stretched his smile like a hand, to her mother, who turned a face lit by gratitude for Coriola's forgiveness. And Coriola turned her own face to her daughter, seeking forgiveness: her daughter, who sat by her bed with a full belly as Coriola sits by her mother's bed, and yet beckoned to her and turned, inevitably, for forgiveness to the child yet unborn who was already, beyond time, seeking forgiveness of her child. And at that moment, in the presence of all fathers, all brothers, in the sight of the completion of all stories, turning veiled un-seeing eyes from side to side on the morning of her death, Coriola saw the wonder, the shadow of death on the pave-ment, the doctor, the vision of Tom, William, the first orgasm, the pushing of life from the womb, all the miracles of intervention that had compelled her to choose life, not the accidents of nature that had lured her towards death; and knew that as her mother poured water on her face, she had been in some way marked, sealed to contend daily with the mystery, the time-bound contradiction of body and soul, the misery of the riding instructress empty and sightless, Fanian standing with his back to her even outside time, the leers of lust frozen on faces for all eter-nity—and she knew the necessity for an unhappiness that would lead to this realization; she knew beyond doubt the necessity for it, though there were not and never could be words to explain it. She feared in an instant for any child who like her would wrestle with mystery, and in that same instant saw the smile on the face of all those children so called, from the beginning to the end of time—and there was only light.

or perhaps, she thought, waiting for the rattle to fade, perhaps, she writes at her desk at forty-one, perhaps she's invented them all, mother, daughter, Tom, William, Fan-ian. Maybe there is just the orderly, threading his way among the white beds, pausing to help a nurse pull the white screen across one of the white beds where a body lies, released from its spirit. Finally at rest.

ABOUT THE AUTHOR

M. J. FITZGERALD was born in New York in 1950 and lived in Italy from the age of three until she was sent to school in England in 1964. She received a B.A. in English from Sussex University (England) and a B.Phil. in Medieval Studies from York University. She has worked as a freelance publisher's reader and translator as well as teaching part time in tutorial colleges and adult education institutes. Between September 1984 and September 1985 she was Southern Arts Writer-in-Residence in Southampton, England. She is the author of a collection of stories, *Rope-Dancer*, and a script for British television, *A Summer Ghost*.